AGAINST ALL ODDS

Eleanor Seymour is under pressure to marry for money, thanks to her father's extravagance. Plagued by an undeserved reputation as a fortune hunter, she must endure the advances of the wealthy but elderly Mr Burnley and the snubs of the aloof James Trentham. But then the shocking climax of an evening at Vauxhall Pleasure Gardens offers her a glimpse into Trentham's secret past. Who is the mysterious woman that haunts him? And can Eleanor believe a single word he says?

JASMINA SVENNE

AGAINST ALL ODDS

Complete and Unabridged

LINFORD
Leicester

First published in Great Britain in 2004

First Linford Edition
published 2005

Copyright © 2004 by Jasmina Svenne
All rights reserved

British Library CIP Data

Svenne, Jasmina M.
    Against all odds.—Large print ed.—
Linford romance library
1. Love stories
2. Large type books
I. Title
823.9′2 [F]

ISBN 1–84395–697–7

Published by
F. A. Thorpe (Publishing)
Anstey, Leicestershire

Set by Words & Graphics Ltd.
Anstey, Leicestershire
Printed and bound in Great Britain by
T. J. International Ltd., Padstow, Cornwall

This book is printed on acid-free paper

1

'Put on your best cap and gown, Eleanor,' Mr Seymour announced as he entered the gloomy drawing-room and dropped into his usual chair. 'If you're not grateful after this, you never will be.'

'What is it, Papa? Where are we going?'

Eleanor Seymour, who had been darning by the window, tried to look grateful, but she was unsure how well she succeeded. There were things preying on her mind and from that point of view she was glad of a distraction. On the other hand . . .

'Mrs Gregory has invited both of us to accompany her to Vauxhall Pleasure Gardens.'

He leaned back in his chair and beamed, obviously expecting his daughter to fling her arms round his neck in delight. Instead, the contrary creature sat with her head bowed, abstractedly rolling her darning needle between her fingers.

'Well, aren't you pleased?' he went on regardless.

'Yes, Papa,' she said dutifully, still not putting away her work.

'Well, well, hurry along. We mustn't keep Mrs Gregory waiting, must we?'

'No, Papa.'

She tucked her work into her basket, but just as she reached the door, she paused and turned back.

'What is it, for goodness' sake?' her father snapped.

'It's only, can we afford it?'

'Can we what?' Mr Seymour's tone crescendoed dangerously.

'The butcher was here this morning, saying he wouldn't let the debt run any longer unless I gave him something on account.'

'Damned impudence. I hope you sent him away with a flea in his ear.'

'I sent him away,' she replied slowly, 'with five shillings I'd saved for a new pair of shoes.'

'Five shillings! Five shillings!'

Mr Seymour was beside himself now, his usually pale face slashed with crimson.

'He wouldn't take any less.'

'Of course he wouldn't if he knew you had that much in your purse. If you behave like a green goose, tradesmen will always take advantage.'

Eleanor, who knew much more of the matter than her father, would not be shifted.

'The man has a right to his money, since we have eaten his meat,' she said mildly. 'He has a wife and three small children to feed.'

'How old are you, Eleanor, that you still believe such fairy stories?'

She said nothing. She had seen the butcher's wife trudging along with a basket on one arm, a baby on the other and two larger children with runny noses staggering after her. Her father would scarcely have recognised the butcher, even if he had met him with his bloodied apron and a cleaver in his hand. She waited patiently while her father ranted. If she tried to leave the room now, he would only follow her upstairs. The servants knew enough of their business already. They didn't need to overhear any more. Her father turned on her suddenly.

'How many times must I explain it to you?' he demanded. 'If you pinch and scrape and let the whole world know you are in a pickle, how many wealthy suitors do you think you are likely to attract? None!'

She knew it would be unwise to point out that her father's system of living on credit for the last five months had not produced any either, so she held her tongue.

'Unless you are seen in the right places with the right people, dressed in the height of fashion, you will never meet anyone eligible.'

His tone softened, a good sign, though sometimes a deceptive one.

'Can't you see that everything I do is for your own good? Not to mention the fact that behaving furtively is liable to bring a whole pack of bailiffs down on us because they'll think we can't pay.'

'Well, we can't.'

It was only a statement of fact, but Mr Seymour interpreted her words as criticism of his actions and exploded.

'Are you calling your father a liar and a thief?'

This was too much.

'I never called you a thief, sir.'

'No? Well, what else is it, to take goods with no intention of paying for them, eh? Let me tell you, I'll pay every single debt I have in the world when I am in better frame.'

Translated, this meant as soon as she was married. Eleanor had come to suspect that it was only the rumours her father spread about her supposedly imminent marriage to one wealthy man or another that had hitherto kept the bailiffs from their door.

'You think I can't pay the entrance fee at Vauxhall? Is that it? You want money for shoes? Here, have some. I've plenty.'

He pulled out a handful of loose change from the deep pockets of his frockcoat, allowing the coins to trickle through his fingers and bounce, spin and roll across the polished surface of the rosewood table. Eleanor tried not to look, afraid of how mercenary she felt at that moment. There was money there to mend her old shoes, buy new ribbons for her gowns and hats, subscribe to the circulating library. Money, even, to give to the grocer on account and pay some of the arrears they owed the servants.

But she knew it was an empty gesture. It was probably all the ready cash her father had in the world. He had always kept his financial matters a secret from her and her mother, assuring them there was no need to addle their delicate female brains over such paltry matters. It was only since her mother's death that Eleanor had even become aware they were not as well off as her father liked to pretend.

She despised herself for noticing that one stray coin bounced off the table and rolled beneath her father's chair. She hoped it was a shilling, and that she would be able to return when the room was empty and pick it up before one of the servants found it. Not that they could be blamed if they did help themselves when they had the opportunity!

'What are you waiting for? Didn't you hear me tell you to go and get ready? And mind, I want you to wear your prettiest smile all night.'

'I wasn't sure if you still wished to go.'

'Wish? Oh, my wishes have nothing to do with it. Miss will have her own way in everything. I suppose you're still pining after that Williams fellow. I've seen how cool you are with some of the men who'd marry you if you had the sense to encourage them.'

Instead of replying, Eleanor edged a vase to the centre of a small table.

'I was right to forbid it,' Mr Seymour insisted. 'You would have been perpetually short of money if you had married him. You ought to have more pride than to wear the willow for something that happened five years ago.'

'I assure you, Papa, I very rarely think of Mr Williams any more.'

Eleanor turned and left the room, not trusting herself to keep her temper if she stayed a moment longer.

When she was ready, she dismissed the maid, and paused a moment longer in front of the mirror. She imagined the overall effect would please her father, although she felt vaguely dissatisfied. Her gown was a polonaise, bunched up at the back and open at the front to show the matching petticoat. Her father insisted on her wearing white, believing it would make her look younger but he was unaware how difficult it was to keep clean. She rubbed her fingernail thoughtfully across a yellowish stain on her bodice, about the size and shape of a teardrop, but it wouldn't shift.

Her round cheeks made her look younger than twenty-five. Her reddish-brown hair was arranged as simply as possible. Papa had even forbidden hair powder, fearing it would make her look too sophisticated.

'Remember, no man is going to notice you if he thinks you are older than eighteen. And don't breathe a word about your real age, unless you want to be left on the shelf.'

Eleanor had frequent rebellious urges, when she wanted to do the exact opposite of what he said, but it seemed wrong to spend money on clothes and hair powder, simply to spite her father, when he could not, or would not, pay for the food they consumed. The thought of marriage was not altogether unappealing, if she could find the right man. What other choice was there for a girl with a genteel education and no money?

She had no rich, heirless relatives to leave her a legacy and her father wouldn't hear of her becoming a governess. If she went behind his back, someone would have to recommend her and it would inevitably come to his ears. Maybe his creditors would hear of it, too, and demand immediate payment when they realised there would be no prosperous son-in-law.

She was tired of living on her wits, constantly moving between the homes of her father's friends and hired lodgings, never knowing from day to day if her father was about to be imprisoned for debt. Eleanor sighed and wished again he had not brought up the painful topic of her first love.

She had been twenty, only a year short of her majority, when she met John Williams. Unfortunately, he had three unmarried sisters and a widowed mother to support. Her dowry had proved inadequate and her father and Mrs Williams were adamant. Eleanor had still been young and impetuous then. Her father would never know how close she came to eloping, but her mother talked her out of it. She assured Eleanor that one year was all she had to endure before she could marry as she pleased.

Her sufferings at that time paled into insignificance beside what she felt when John Williams got engaged to a wealthier woman instead. He married her only a month before Eleanor's twenty-first birthday. As if to spite her, two of his sisters had also made good matches since then without their brother's assistance.

She picked up her candle and made her way downstairs. The house was too large for two people, but it was a part of her father's strategy of keeping up appearances. If Eleanor had had her way, they would have taken a smaller house in an unfashionable part of London and dismissed the footman and at least one of the three maids, but none of the money was hers and fretting about it wouldn't help.

The drawing-room was empty, as she knew it would be. Her father might make jokes about how long it took women to get ready, but he always spent more time on his toilette than Eleanor did on hers. She stooped by her father's chair and ran her fingers tentatively over the carpet. Sure enough, there it was. She scooped up the coin and took it to the light to make certain, but she guessed from its size it was only a sixpence, not to be sneered at by any means, but not as much as she had hoped for.

She had just managed to conceal it when her father entered, looking urbane in his evening suit of blue silk, embroidered with silver thread. He had powdered his hair to hide the grey streaks in it. Although he was the wrong side of fifty, it was not immediately obvious to the casual observer. Since he came out of mourning, there had been rumours of a possible second marriage, ostensibly to acquire a suitable chaperone for his daughter. Only the puckers between his eyebrows revealed to Eleanor that she was still in disfavour with him, but they reached Mrs Gregory's house without any further quarrels.

As always, they were punctual and as

always, Mrs Gregory kept them waiting. She and her more favoured guests were still dining and Eleanor could hear animated voices and bursts of laughter coming from the dining-room. The drawing-room, into which they were shown, was a blaze of light.

Mrs Gregory's drawing-room intimidated Eleanor, with its high, painted ceiling and its expanse of rose-spattered carpet between clumps of chairs and sofas. Everything from the largest urn to the smallest pawn of the ivory chess set had been placed so it would catch the light. At long last she heard voices approaching.

'Ah, Seymour, I hope you haven't been waiting long,' Mrs Gregory said in the slightly too loud tones of someone who is growing deaf, as he bowed over the two fingers she offered him. 'What's that? Speak up, if you please. So many people seem to mumble nowadays.'

'I said I would be willing to wait an eternity for you,' Mr Seymour replied in booming tones.

Eleanor had been trying to keep to the shadows until Mrs Gregory was ready to speak to her, but the white dress thwarted her plan. A voice close beside her made her jump.

'Aha, so you are here after all. I knew you couldn't be far if your father was about.'

Her cheek muscles froze.

'Good evening, sir,' she said curtseying and trying to ignore the way in which Mr Burnley, an elderly man with waistcoat buttons straining at their holes, was ogling her.

True to form, Mr Burnley held out a large, greasy-looking hand and asked, 'Why so formal, Miss Seymour, with an old friend?'

He chuckled to demonstrate he did not consider himself to be too old to flirt with a girl young enough to be his granddaughter. Eleanor was forced to submit to the inevitable and let him grasp her fingers.

'That's better, more friendly,' he said, ignoring Eleanor's surreptitious attempt to draw her hand free again. 'How utterly bewitching you look tonight, like a bride at her wedding feast.'

'Thank you,' Eleanor murmured, her eyes flicking round the room for someone to save her.

Mr Burnley added his other hand, crushing her fingers from all sides.

'You're not planning to elope tonight, I hope, under the cover of darkness.'

'If I were, I would be most unwise to confess it now, wouldn't I?'

A younger man was loitering nearby. The sight of him made her heart beat faster. If Mr Trentham offered to shake hands with her, Mr Burnley would have to let go. She managed to catch Trentham's eye. Ever since their first meeting, Eleanor had thought he had rather striking eyes, vivid, cornflower blue with strong eyebrows. But there was no friendly gleam in them on this occasion.

She ought to have known better. He merely bowed frigidly and muttered, 'Your servant, madam.'

She only managed to free her hand when Mrs Gregory turned to her. Like a child, she wanted to wipe it clean on her petticoat and keep her fingers tightly locked behind her back so Mr Burnley couldn't take hold of them again. The ordeal of getting into the carriage was still ahead of her. By daylight she might have managed the steps without assistance, but the light was fading and it was a matter of etiquette.

Mrs Gregory was one of those ladies who always looked magnificent, whatever she wore, despite her plumpness. She had chaperoned Eleanor a good deal throughout the season, partly because she was flattered by Mr Seymour's attentions, and partly to annoy various nephews and nieces, who hoped to be mentioned in her will.

'Turn around, child,' Mrs Gregory said. 'Let me see you properly.'

Eleanor obeyed, but blushed deeply when she caught Mr Trentham's satirical gaze.

'Yes, you'll do. White always looks proper on a young lady,' Mrs Gregory announced. 'Your mother's jewels, I suppose?'

She pointed at Eleanor's necklace with a lace-trimmed fan.

'Yes,' Eleanor lied, but the blood rushed to her face.

In fact it was an exact copy of the diamond necklace she had inherited from her mother. The original had been sold long ago to pay a particularly insistent landlord.

'You shall ride with me tonight,' Mrs Gregory said, in what was intended to be a whisper.

Eleanor curtsied, feeling the hostile eyes of her hostess's relatives upon her. She didn't like being a pawn in this power game. She also knew that, as the least important member of the group, she would have to ride with her back to the horses, something she ought to be used to by now, but which still sometimes made her nauseous.

Mrs Gregory always insisted on

having the most important gentlemen in her carriage, which, in this case, probably meant Mr Trentham and Mr Burnley. One of them would have to sit beside Eleanor and she had the horrible feeling it would be Mr Burnley.

2

Mrs Gregory was helped into the carriage first. Eleanor followed and drew herself as far into the corner as she could, inwardly cursing the width of her gown. She didn't want to crease it, but even less did she relish the prospect of having to drape it across the knees of whichever gentleman finally won the privilege of riding backwards beside her. Mr Burnley and Mr Trentham were still discussing the matter, each trying to outdo the other in politeness and deference.

'I really must insist, sir,' Mr Trentham's voice was growing dangerously impatient.

'Perhaps Mrs Gregory should be the one to settle this dispute.'

Eleanor was startled to hear her father's voice. She had assumed he had already taken his place in one of the other vehicles. His suggestion was instantly seized upon by the company and the old lady seemed pleased at being chosen as the arbiter of good manners.

'I am afraid I must agree with Mr Trentham,' she announced at length, having enjoyed her position of power as long as she could. 'It would set a dangerous precedent, don't you think, if I were to slight the claims of age over wealth?'

Eleanor had not realised she was holding her breath until that moment. Mr Burnley took his seat next to Mrs Gregory with ill-concealed disappointment and consoled himself with a pinch of snuff and a leer in Eleanor's direction.

Once Mr Trentham was in his place, the steps were folded, the door shut and the carriage lurched into motion. The iron-rimmed wheels clattered on the cobblestones, making conversation almost impossible. Eleanor felt acutely aware of Mr Trentham's silent figure beside her.

She couldn't help remember a different carriage ride, some months ago, coming home from a ball. She had been so deliciously happy, she had feigned sleep in order to be left alone with her thoughts. But Mrs Gregory, who had chaperoned her that night, kept talking to her father. Her voice was so loud, it intruded into Eleanor's waking dreams. At the time she had been all too willing to listen to anyone discuss this particular topic. How young and foolish she had been then, only four or five months ago.

'Oh, yes, Mr James Trentham is worth cultivating,' Mrs Gregory had said. 'A very comfortable fortune, five thousand a year, and the most charming house in the whole of Nottinghamshire.'

Eleanor had known for years that five thousand a year was far more than a girl with no expectations could hope for, and yet greater miracles sometimes happened, especially if the gentleman was not encumbered with younger siblings to provide for. Mr Trentham had danced with her that evening and had given her no reason to believe he disliked her.

However, the next time she had met him at the theatre, he cut her dead, as if he had never seen her before, and rebuffed her shy smile with a cool stare. At the first opportunity, he made his excuses and left Mrs Gregory's box. At first Eleanor had been hurt, but she hoped there was some misunderstanding that could be quickly cleared up. Perhaps he had just forgotten. No matter how mortifying that might be to her pride, it was better than the alternative, that he didn't want to remember her. But as the weeks passed and Mr Trentham remained aloof, her pain turned to anger, which she was forced to swallow because of her lowly position.

The traffic was now growing heavier as they trundled across Westminster Bridge and as they approached Vauxhall, they slowed nearly to a standstill.

'That's the worst thing about Vauxhall,' Mrs Gregory sighed, fanning herself languidly, 'They'll let virtually anyone inside, especially on a fine night like this.'

'Perhaps someone important is expected tonight,' Eleanor suggested. 'The Prince of Wales maybe.'

She did not care much about such things, but she knew Mrs Gregory set great store by seeing as many famous people as possible.

'What's that, child? Speak up.'

'Miss Seymour said she'd like to meet the Prince of Wales,' Trentham replied in her place.

He had an unusually clear voice, which carried even when he made no apparent effort to raise it. Eleanor flushed.

'Indeed, sir, I said nothing of the kind,' she began, but Mrs Gregory interrupted her.

'Oh, so you want to see the prince, do you? Just beware he doesn't fall in love with that pretty face of yours.'

'I think that is rather too ambitious, even for a Seymour,' Trentham muttered under his breath.

Eleanor drew in her breath, stung to the core. Angry words were on her lips and she bit them back with difficulty. Why did Trentham despise her so much that he had forgotten his customary good manners? It was so unfair. She couldn't even fight back because of who she was.

Neither of the other occupants of the carriage seemed to have heard his sarcastic remark. Eleanor seethed silently while Mrs Gregory and Mr Burnley discussed the shocking behaviour of the princes, the beauty of the princesses and the frugality of the king and queen. She must find some way in which to revenge herself on Trentham.

At long last they reached their destination. The gentlemen scrambled out in order to help them descend. Eleanor could hardly repress a shudder when she was forced to place her hand in Mr Burnley's again and she glanced instinctively over her shoulder to see if there was any sign of her father and the rest of the party.

'There, now, Miss Seymour, you've nothing to fear,' the elderly gentleman said, tucking her hand through his arm with a self-satisfied smile. 'I shall take care you don't become lost.'

He kept his free hand clasped over her fingers, as if afraid she might escape, despite the bustle and confusion around them. It was by no means Eleanor's first visit to Vauxhall, but Mr Burnley pointed out all the sights, the Chinese pavilion, the supper boxes, the octagonal bandstand, as if she had only just arrived from the country. She guessed that Mr Burnley wanted to draw her away from the rest of the group, into one of the tree-lined alleys, where lanterns were scattered at wide intervals. It was not quite midsummer and it was not completely dark yet outdoors, and for that Eleanor was profoundly grateful.

Her father had somehow found his way to Mrs Gregory's side, along with other hangers-on eager to do her bidding. Eleanor tried to signal to him how desperate she was to escape her present companion, but he ignored her. Trentham seemed to have disappeared already, not, of course, that he would lift a finger to save her.

'And at nine o'clock,' Mr Burnley said, bringing Eleanor back to her immediate surroundings, 'a bell rings and the illuminations begin.'

'Yes, I know. I've seen them before,' Eleanor replied, too distracted and uncomfortable to pretend any longer.

Mr Burnley looked put out for a moment. He was about to turn the incident into a joke, by pretending she had been deceiving him rather than admitting he had made assumptions about her, when a group of his acquaintances came into view. Eleanor felt she could have almost kissed a stranger if he or she saved her from having to spend any more time alone with Mr Burnley. She hardly knew anyone there and no-one took any notice of her. Could it do any harm if she just stepped aside a little, nearer to the bandstand, so she could hear the music? After all, she wouldn't lose sight of them and could quickly return when they started moving.

The temptation was too strong for Eleanor. She edged away from Mr Burnley. To her surprise, she discovered he was so preoccupied, talking to a thin gentleman, he didn't notice. At first she was alert, checking every two seconds to make sure the others were still there, but the music wove its spell on her and she was only roused when a strange voice suddenly boomed in her ear.

'Are you here on your own, my beauty?'

She turned and flinched, almost overpowered by the smell of alcohol on the young man's breath.

'No, my friends are just over there.'

Her voice faded as she glanced back and realised the little group was no longer where she had left them.

'Are you lost? Never mind, sweet-heart. I'll look after you. I know some good places where we could look.'

He thinks I am a woman of ill repute, she thought with a shudder. She had to get rid of him and find Mrs Gregory's party. Every moment she stood there talking to him, they might be getting farther and farther away.

'Excuse me. I really must go,' she said hurriedly.

'What will you give me if I help find your friends?' he persisted. 'Now, don't be unkind, darling.'

She began walking as fast as she could without breaking into a run, but the man followed her. It was almost completely dark by now which made it difficult to recognise anyone from a distance. Whatever else she did, she was resolved she wouldn't let this stranger tempt her into any of the alleys. She must keep to the light.

She thought she caught sight of her father's blue coat and hurried towards the supper boxes on the other side of the piazza.

'What's your hurry, sweetheart? The night is still young,' her companion panted, taking her by the arm.

'Let go of me, sir,' she said, winced and twisted free of him.

The man in the blue coat turned and Eleanor's steps faltered. It wasn't her father and she was more completely lost than ever. Perhaps they hadn't yet realised she was missing, each member of the group assuming she was with somebody else.

They could have gone anywhere. If they had missed her, perhaps they were looking for her near the bandstand, where they had last seen her. How would she ever know where to search? The gardens were too vast and already her feet were beginning to hurt in her high-heeled shoes.

Eleanor had never been aware of how many strangers there were in London. Why couldn't she stumble upon someone she had met at a party or danced with at a ball, even if she couldn't find Mrs Gregory's group immediately? Instead it was her unwelcome companion who was suddenly hailed by a friend.

'Well, well, Harry, what have you found here?'

He was just as drunk as Harry, judging from the fumes he emitted and the jaunty roll in his gait.

'Just a poor little waif who has lost her friends. I'm helping her find them,' he said with a knowing wink.

It was her last chance to escape. They were closing in on her, one on either side, and pretty soon it would be too late. Eleanor backed away from them, turned, and began to run. Neither of them had been expecting this, which gave Eleanor the advantage of a head start. But, fired up by the wine and spirits they had consumed, the chase only whetted their appetites and they were soon close on her tail.

She ran along the full length of the arcade hoping desperately to see someone she knew. She was so frantic she hardly looked where she was going. She wouldn't be able to keep this pace up for long. Her heels wobbled dangerously, threatening to twist her ankle. A man turned at the sound of her steps and for a moment she didn't recognise him.

'Miss Seymour!' he exclaimed.

'Oh, Mr Trentham, thank goodness,' she gasped, tempted to fling herself upon his breast, despite the fact he was not alone, but the cool tones in which he replied soon dissipated that urge.

'What on earth are you doing here by yourself?'

Eleanor was too breathless to reply. She recognised the men with him as his closest friends. It looked as if they had been discussing serious business before she had interrupted them. She glanced back at her pursuers.

There was no sign of the second man, but the one he had called Harry was nearby. He marched straight up to them and announced, 'Excuse me, gentlemen, but I think I have first claim to this prize.'

This time he clenched her arm so tightly, it was all she could do to prevent herself from crying out in pain.

It was a threat as much as anything else. He wouldn't deal gently with her if he were allowed to drag her off somewhere.

'And who might you be, sir?' Trentham said in his haughtiest tones.

Harry was too drunk to be intimidated so easily.

'I'm the man who found this pretty little wench first and I think I've a right to keep her,' he announced, jutting out his chin.

'Indeed? Even if this pretty little wench is a respectable young lady?'

The drunk took a step back, dropping Eleanor's arm. Trentham's blue eyes bore into him and even his fuddled brain was beginning to suspect he had made a mistake. He began floundering for words, but Trentham ignored him and turned to his friends.

'Excuse me a moment while I escort Miss Seymour back to Mrs Gregory,' he said.

Obediently, Eleanor slipped her hand through the crook of his arm. She was still wheezing, her heart pounding, and she could hardly keep up with him as he strode away.

'I gather you have had an unpleasant experience,' Mr Trentham remarked. 'Who is that fellow?'

'I don't know. He just came up to me and he kept following me when I was trying to find the others.'

'How did you come to be alone in the first place?' he persisted.

'I was listening to the music and I didn't notice when they moved on.'

His face didn't soften one jot and he snorted contemptuously.

'I would have expected better from a well-brought up young lady.'

Though she knew he was right, she searched for a point of attack.

'I am perfectly aware that you think I am not well brought up,' she declared, emboldened by the fact there weren't witnesses. 'Whereas, of course, your manners are always impeccable, even towards someone as far beneath your notice as myself.'

Even through his sleeve, Eleanor could feel the muscles in his arm tighten as he clenched his fists, but he said nothing. He was staring straight ahead and so he did not see a noisy little troop pass them. Eleanor would scarcely have noticed them either, but for one thing.

Catching sight of Trentham's face in the lamplight, one of the strangers stopped abruptly. Eleanor got an impression of a young woman, too pale to look healthy, with large, dark eyes. She averted her gaze. Somehow she felt it would have been an invasion to look at this stranger too closely. There was a brooding air of unhappiness about her.

Mr Trentham paused to consult his watch.

'We had better hurry if we wish to see the illuminations,' he said with a note of relief. 'I should think that is where we will find the others.'

'Just as you please,' Eleanor replied haughtily, but when they reached the cascade, she forgot her bad temper and was as enchanted as a child, watching the display.

Mr Trentham managed to ensure good places for them, but in the throng it had been impossible to locate the rest of their party.

'Oh, here they are. Mr Trentham!'

Eleanor turned at the sound of her father's voice. Mr Seymour was bearing down on them with Mrs Gregory on his arm. His smug smile made Eleanor's heart sink. He thought she had snared a rich prize. Perhaps as early as tomorrow he might be whispering to his friends and creditors about five thousand a year.

And then it happened. It was all over so quickly, even Eleanor, who had the clearest view, did not realise its significance for the first few minutes. The pale girl she had glimpsed as they had passed them earlier appeared out of nowhere and lunged at Mr Trentham, hissing something in a low tone. At the same time, something snapped with a metallic sound. Eleanor saw a look of shocked recognition in Trentham's eyes.

'Louisa,' he gasped, snatching her arm. 'Wait!'

The woman tore herself free and vanished into the darkness of the nearest alley. Eleanor's father started forward to pursue her, but Trentham grabbed him by the sleeve.

'Let her go.'

'It's no trouble.'

'I don't want a scandal.'

'But she robbed you.'

'No, she didn't.'

A grim smile twisted Trentham's lips and he glanced down at his chest, where the woman had struck him.

'I want this kept quiet.'

'I'll be discretion itself,' Mr Seymour tossed the last words over his shoulder before he disappeared into the darkness.

Mr Trentham seemed tempted to follow and only remembered about the ladies at the last minute. His eyes gazed anxiously down the alley in which the fugitives had disappeared.

'What in heaven's name is happening?' Mrs Gregory demanded.

For a reply, Mr Trentham removed the hand he had instinctively clutched to his chest and Eleanor saw the first thin smear of blood soaking through his shirt.

3

Neither Mrs Gregory nor Eleanor screamed. Apparently gaining confidence from this, Trentham spoke in a quiet voice that shook only the tiniest fraction.

'Don't alarm anyone. I want this kept quiet.'

Mrs Gregory seemed to understand.

'But shouldn't we call for assistance?' she quavered.

'No. I'm not badly hurt. Let's find a more secluded spot. Don't look so alarmed, madam. I'll explain when we are alone.'

Eleanor knew this hint referred to her, but Mrs Gregory needed help, even if Mr Trentham did not. The old lady was beginning to look unsteady on her feet and, though she felt as if her own legs had been filled with icy water, Eleanor gave Mrs Gregory her arm to lean on.

They followed Mr Trentham to a quiet alley. He paused beneath a lamp and undid the top button of his waistcoat. He peeled it back gingerly, as if he was unsure what he would discover.

'A mere scratch,' he said, letting out a shuddering breath. 'The blade broke on my button, I think.'

'Blade? Good gracious, man, how can you say that so calmly?' Mrs Gregory demanded.

Eleanor, eager to be of assistance, offered him her handkerchief to help stem the bleeding. He applied it to the wound. It was a little more than a scratch, Eleanor judged, not life-threatening.

'Do you think she'll try again?' she asked, her voice shaking.

'No, absolutely not. Why couldn't Seymour just let her go?'

'I'm sure my father was only trying to help.'

Eleanor drew away from him sharply, repelled by his ingratitude.

'Don't upset yourself,' Mrs Gregory said and patted Trentham on the arm. 'Seymour is a very useful man to have around and he knows when to hold his tongue. He may be a cat's-paw, but he does have his uses.'

Eleanor was mortified. She knew her father had his faults, but he was her father nonetheless and her closest living relative. And the worst of it was, she would not have been surprised to discover her father believed the people who made use of him genuinely liked him.

'I should go and see what has become of him,' Trentham said, stirring impatiently, 'but I can hardly leave you unattended.'

'Mr Burnley said he would go and secure us a supper box,' Mrs Gregory said. 'We agreed to meet there if we should get separated again.'

Trentham offered them an arm each and led them back to the brighter lights. But the group they found in the piazza, consisting of Mr Burnley and an assortment of Mrs Gregory's relatives, had a dejected air.

All the supper boxes in the nearest arcade were already taken. Eleanor was beginning to feel the strain of being on her feet for so long and the older members of the party were probably even more weary. They trudged to the opposite side of the piazza, but they had no luck in the second arcade either.

'Oh,' Mrs Gregory said impatiently, 'if Mr Seymour were here, he would manage something.'

'How very tiresome,' one of her nieces said. 'Always pestering and boring one when he isn't needed, and when he is, not a sign of him.'

Eleanor's tongue burned to make some kind of retort, but all these people were her elders and betters. She had no idea how long it would be before she could escape from Vauxhall and go home.

'I'll go and see if I can find him,' Trentham said, leaving Mr Burnley with the party of irate females, in spite of their protests.

Since none of those present would have dreamed of abusing someone as influential as Mr Trentham, it was Eleanor's father on whom they vented their feelings for a good ten or fifteen minutes before someone noticed a vacated supper box. They managed to claim it before anyone else got there and dropped wearily into the seats.

Sick at heart, Eleanor could not touch a morsel. Her father had gone after a madwoman and instead of being concerned for his safety, these people were abusing him and laughing at his willingness to perform menial tasks for them in exchange for an invitation or a small loan. She began to shiver as the chill of evening deepened. After what seemed like hours, Mr Trentham finally returned alone.

'No luck?' Mr Burnley asked.

'Yes. Mr Seymour sends word that he has been unavoidably forced to leave, but that we should not curtail our pleasures on his account.'

Trentham delivered the message with the air of having memorised it, but Eleanor detected a sneer in his voice. Perhaps he was mocking the pleasure seekers as well as or instead of her father, but by then she was sensitive to the slightest insult.

'Didn't he send any message for me?' she asked.

'I'm afraid not.'

She felt Mr Burnley's eyes turn towards her and her cheeks burned.

'Well!' one of the ladies declared. 'Fancy abandoning his own daughter like that in a public place.'

'I daresay he thought her safe enough under Mrs Gregory's care,' Mr Burnley hastened to intervene.

Why was it only now that they remembered who she was, and not earlier when they could have spared her some unnecessary pain by refraining from discussing her father in such tones? Eleanor was desperate to get back home. She was utterly dependent on the whims of the others. If they chose to stay till two or three in the morning, she would have to stay, too.

Luckily the party, though somewhat refreshed, was unable to recapture its earlier high spirits. Mrs Gregory was physically tired, Mr Burnley annoyed that for a large part of the evening Eleanor had managed to evade him and had returned on Trentham's arm, and the nephews and nieces had obviously quarrelled among themselves at some point.

Mr Trentham was urged to sit down and have some supper. He declined any food, but as he sank into an empty seat beside Eleanor, she noticed there was a faint dew of sweat upon his forehead and upper lip, suggesting his wound was giving him more pain than he would admit. Surreptitiously, he pulled out a handkerchief — Eleanor was pretty sure it was hers from the dark stain in one corner — and mopped his face when he thought no-one was watching.

Moved by pity, she asked in a low

voice, 'Are you quite well, sir?'

'Perfectly,' he replied with a frown.

Offended at being rebuffed again and mortified because he must have thought she was indiscreet rather than softhearted, Eleanor fell into silence.

Eventually they rose and wandered about a bit longer, before they conceded defeat. The others squabbled over who would travel in which carriage. Luckily there was one place left for her in Mrs Gregory's carriage.

'Has my father been back long?' Eleanor asked as the footman let her in.

Her eyes fell on the table. There was no sign of her father's hat and his gold-topped cane was not in its customary corner.

'The master hasn't returned yet,' the footman replied.

Feeling she ought to give some explanation, she added, 'He had to go on an errand for someone, so naturally I assumed . . . I don't suppose he will be much longer.'

All her anxiety for her father's safety

returned in full force. Was he still alive? If that woman had stabbed him with greater accuracy than she had Trentham, could he have bled to death in one of those secluded alleys before someone found him? She tried to reassure herself that Trentham had apparently seen him safe and well, but she couldn't disguise the fact he had looked shaken by the whole ordeal.

She wanted to sit up and wait for news, but that would have meant keeping her maid up, too. Instead, bidding the footman to wait for his master, she retired to her room to remove her finery. She knew full well that she would get no sleep and after Dinah, the maid, had left, she sat by the window, listening.

In the loneliness and quiet, there was plenty of time to ask questions. Trentham clearly knew this woman and why she had attacked him. Obviously it was not a tale that would be much to his credit if it did become public knowledge.

For a moment Eleanor wove fantasies of avenging herself on Trentham, by making allusions to his secret in public, teasing him, forcing him to dance with her and be polite to her. Then she sighed and gave up. It was no good. She couldn't imagine herself behaving so unscrupulously, no matter what Trentham had done to her.

Noises from the street became less and less frequent, till only the occasional carriage rattled by. If anything had happened to her father, surely somebody would have sent for her.

She was sliding into a drowse, when the rap finally came at the door. Wrapping her robe tighter around herself, she glided on to the landing, her hands slippery on the banister as she leaned over it. She was suddenly afraid. Suppose it was not her father at the door?

At the sight of the familiar figure, she hurled herself downstairs.

'Eleanor! What the devil . . . '

'Oh, Papa, I wasn't sure if you were safe.'

'Hush!'

Eleanor brought herself hastily under control. Her father seemed unhurt. Not even his cravat was ruffled.

'You ought to be in bed, Nell.'

She was not deceived. Her father only ever called her Nell if he was pleased with her or himself.

'Where have you been?' she asked with suppressed excitement.

Mr Seymour smiled blandly.

'Arranging matters for Mr Trentham. That's all you need to know.'

'But, Papa . . . '

'That's all you need to know, for the moment,' Mr Seymour repeated firmly, but Eleanor could see a smile on his lips. 'Except . . . '

A broad grin spread across his face.

'This night's work may be the making of us yet,' her father said, rubbing his hands. 'Mr Trentham has invited us to spend the summer at his house in Nottinghamshire.'

★　★　★

48

'There it is, Deepwater Hall,' Mrs Gregory announced.

Eleanor, who had been travelling backwards the whole way from the inn at Leicester, where they had spent a restless night, leaned forward and craned her neck to see out of the window.

She was not sure what she had expected, but as soon as she saw it, it struck her as the perfect house for James Trentham. It had columns on either side of the front door and symmetrical sash windows gilded by the evening sun. Foreboding settled more determinedly in the pit of her stomach. She had been uneasy ever since her father's triumphant return from Vauxhall that evening and seeing the house in which she was to pass the next weeks confirmed her darkest fears. It was far too grand and she couldn't persuade her father she would never be its mistress.

Ostensibly they were travelling as part of Mrs Gregory's retinue, her father acting as courier along the way, arranging changes of horses and procuring the best beds and food available. He was in his element. Now they had arrived, Eleanor had no doubt he would change his rôle to a sort of honorary footman, fetching and carrying, soothing minor irritations and generally making himself indispensable to anyone with power, rank or money.

Mr Seymour had been absent for long periods, on business, in the days before their departure and her father evaded all Eleanor's questions about the woman at Vauxhall. He had produced mysterious sums of money with which Eleanor paid off the most pressing bills, including the wages of the maids they were leaving behind in London. Her father, intent on making a genteel appearance, insisted on taking Dinah and the footman with them.

The carriage stopped opposite a short flight of steps leading to the front door. Mr Seymour clambered out nimbly to help Mrs Gregory out.

Eleanor waited her turn patiently. She was startled by the sound of Trentham's clear voice, welcoming Mrs Gregory. She was not yet ready to confront him. Since the visit to Vauxhall, she avoided him studiously and was undermined at every turn by her father, who seemed to think there was a promising romance between them.

She expected her father to help her descend, but Mr Seymour had apparently forgotten her existence and was already giving instructions to the servants about which boxes belonged to Mrs Gregory and should therefore be given additional care. Trentham saw Eleanor's hesitation as her foot groped for the step. In an instant, he was beside her, offering his hand. Momentarily their eyes locked, almost on a level, then she dipped down the steps and the gravel crunched beneath her foot.

'Thank you, sir,' she murmured.

Eleanor followed the others into a spacious hall, dominated by a staircase wide enough for a lady in full court dress to sweep down it. It was darker in the house than outdoors, but even so Eleanor caught glimpses of its beauty. What on earth was she doing here?

★　★　★

At the foot of the table, amid the humbler guests, Eleanor felt more at ease than she had expected to in Mr Trentham's house. Mr Burnley was present, but he was at a safe distance at the other end of the table. One of Eleanor's closest friends, Harriet Reed, was sitting nearby so they could exchange mischievous glances. When the ladies rose to leave the gentlemen to their port, Eleanor felt the moist eyes of Mr Burnley follow her to the door. She was only too pleased when Harriet caught hold of her arm and drew her into a dark corner of the drawing-room for a chat.

'How on earth did your father manage it?' Harriet asked after their first greetings were over. 'Mamma made Papa's life a misery until he all but begged Mr Trentham to invite us.'

'I'm not sure,' Eleanor confessed. 'I believe Papa did Mr Trentham a favour, but he won't tell me anything.'

She was tempted to tell Harriet about the night at Vauxhall, but her father as well as Mr Trentham had sworn her to secrecy. Harriet sighed and wriggled her shoulders.

'Wouldn't it be nice to be owed a favour by such a rich man?' she murmured. 'Especially such a hand-some one.'

Coincidentally, the door sprang open at that moment and the object of Harriet's admiration entered with a party of gentlemen. Eleanor noticed her father among the number. He was listening attentively to a prosperous-looking man with what looked like a very expensive snuffbox in his hand.

Candlelight suited Trentham, Eleanor admitted grudgingly. His high forehead, straight nose and firm chin looked as cleanly cut as a cameo against the panelling. He must have been in his mid-thirties, but the glowing light made him look younger by softening the contours of his face.

In spite of her better judgement, she blurted out, 'You had best be careful with him, Harriet. Rich men have a tendency to take advantage of poor women.'

Harriet's eyes stretched into saucers.

'What have you heard?' she asked.

'Nothing,' Eleanor stammered, feeling she had gone too far.

'Did you know he has a ward living here, a little girl? No-one seems to know who her parents are.'

Eleanor suddenly had an image of a pale waif locked in the garret and guarded by a strict governess. Suppose the woman at Vauxhall was the little girl's mother? If he was deliberately keeping a child away from its mother, no wonder she wanted to kill him. Harriet roused her out of her speculations.

'Here comes your ancient admirer,' she whispered.

4

Eleanor turned her head. Mr Burnley was indeed plodding in their direction. She clutched the lace ruffle on Harriet's sleeve.

'Whatever you do, don't leave me alone with him.'

Many of the younger members of the party were beginning to assemble round the harpsichord and Eleanor wished she could vanish in their midst. But in this, as in everything else in the world, rank and wealth took precedence over talent or enthusiasm.

Mr Burnley seemed only too pleased to have two such enchanting maidens to entertain, as he himself phrased it. Unfortunately, he had not the slightest idea how to go about it. He patronised them by talking about the sorts of frivolous subjects he deemed suitable for young ladies, while they were trying to listen to the music.

Harriet stuck by her like a limpet, but Eleanor could see the longing glances she threw towards the harpsichord. Harriet's one outstanding talent was for music and, because her father was only moderately well off, she had never had the opportunity to play such a fine instrument.

Her face lit up involuntarily when Mr Trentham strolled casually up to them and remarked, 'I trust you will take your turn in entertaining us tonight, Miss Reed.'

Harriet glanced at Eleanor and tried to bring her features under control.

'I was a little hoarse earlier today, so I am not sure it would be wise.'

Her voice was trailing away lamely. Eleanor could not let her do it.

'Couldn't you try just one song?'

The sparkle returned at once to Harriet's eyes, but she bit her lip and threw a lightning glance at Mr Burnley.

'Do you really think I ought to?'

'It would be a mark of ingratitude to

Mr Trentham if you didn't.'

A moment more and she would be left on her own with Mr Burnley. In her panic, Eleanor blurted out the first thing that came into her head to detain Trentham.

'I hear you are a great connoisseur of music, sir.'

He gave her a startled look.

'I know a little about the subject,' he replied, 'and I have been fortunate enough to hear some of the greatest musicians perform, both in London and abroad.'

'How I envy you.'

He was going to get away and Mr Burnley was already trying to butt in.

'Mr Burnley tells me he saw the Mozart children at Ranelagh ten years ago. Were you there, too?'

Eleanor knew she must sound terribly forward, interrupting her elders like that. She tried what a pleading look could do, but it didn't seem to soften Trentham at all.

'Yes, I saw them.'

'Do tell me about it.'

Barely suppressing a sigh, Trentham perched on the edge of a chair.

'I don't quite know what you expect me to say,' he said. 'What I saw was a small girl in a silk gown accompanying a smaller boy in a large, powdered wig.'

'But they did play beautifully, didn't they?'

'Oh, yes, particularly the boy.'

He threw an impatient glance at the harpsichord. The previous song had finished and Harriet had just settled herself on the stool, with the obligatory gentleman leaning over her shoulder to turn the pages for her.

Eleanor correctly interpreted his impatience as the result of his fear that she would talk all the way through her friend's performance. Obligingly she fell silent, leaving Mr Burnley with the opportunity he was waiting for. He began a long and involved explanation of counterpoint, a musical term he obviously didn't understand fully himself. Mr Trentham frowned, but as he directed the frown straight ahead of him and not at the offending party, it had no effect.

Eleanor felt obliged to respond to Mr Burnley by a series of nods, smiles and monosyllables, but it was not enough to appease either gentleman. There was a spontaneous burst of applause as the last note faded away and Mr Burnley joined in, even though he had scarcely heard a note.

'Magnificent voice,' he pronounced secure in the knowledge that no-one would contradict him.

'Very nice, for an amateur,' Mr Trentham said, rousing Eleanor's indignation, 'though I think Miss Reed was right. She is a little hoarse tonight.'

Eleanor's protest died on her lips. In the circumstances, she couldn't exactly say that she had never heard Harriet in better voice. Harriet herself was turning over the music, looking for some other song. In response to something she said, the young man who had been leaning over her shoulder detached himself from the group round the instrument.

There wasn't time for Eleanor to notice any more. Mr Trentham had risen with an excuse and she knew she could not keep him any longer.

'Miss Seymour.'

'Yes?'

Harriet's page-turner made a comical little bow and said, with a grin crinkling his eyes.

'Miss Reed's compliments and would you care to help her out in a duet?'

Harriet, you angel, Eleanor thought.

'Of course, anything to oblige.'

Without a backward glance, Eleanor crossed the room. Performing in public always frightened her, but this time she wouldn't have to do it alone.

'I don't know how to thank you,' she breathed in an undertone as she leaned her head next to Harriet's fair one. Harriet grinned.

'One good turn deserves another.'

'And not a moment too soon. What do you want us to sing?'

During the duet, Eleanor heard her voice quaver here and there, as it never did when she practised alone. She kept her eyes fixed on the music, aware that her father wanted her to shine in front of this illustrious company.

It was easier once she was seated at the harpsichord and had the perfect excuse not to look up. Before she began playing, she glanced round the room. She couldn't see Mr Trentham anywhere and she hoped he had left.

It gave her confidence and she did better than she dared expect, only stumbling twice over difficult passages. The keys were stiffer than on the instrument she usually practised on. But afterwards, while Mrs Gregory was complimenting Harriet on her performance, Eleanor couldn't help overhearing a snatch of conversation.

'Oh, yes, extremely talented,' Mr Trentham agreed with his companion.

'I thought Miss Seymour did well, too.'

Eleanor's heart beat faster.

'If I were you, I would stay well clear of her. That playing is the product of years of drilling with only one aim in mind, to land herself a rich husband.'

She flicked open her fan. She had to cool her face, before somebody noticed. How dare he say such a thing when he hardly knew her? It was true her behaviour might not have been quite proper, but it was the first time she had ever inflicted herself on him and she determined never to do it again.

Trentham turned and caught her eye. She blushed under his gaze and he, too, seemed taken aback for a moment. Then he drew himself upright and stalked away. He would never have admitted it, but the look of shock in Eleanor Seymour's eyes made him deeply uncomfortable. He had been determined not to give her any excuse to accuse him of bad manners again. She was his guest, after all. But somehow he never seemed his usual self in her presence.

His first instinct was to apologise, but

he checked it firmly. Maybe now she would know better than to try her wiles on him. Though, to be fair, this was the first time the girl had made any obvious attempt to attract his attention. Until then, everything had been going well. There had been a few minor troubles, but nothing that could not be hidden from all but the sharpest eyes. Unfortunately, no-one had sharper eyes than the busybody Seymour. There were times when it seemed to Trentham that he could not turn round without finding Seymour standing behind him, humbly offering his assistance.

The man had his uses, of course. Trentham had to admit he would not have had Seymour's patience with Louisa Alcock's wild accusations. She had trusted Seymour and gone with him as docilely as a lamb, when he offered to escort her home from Vauxhall, following the stabbing incident.

It irked Trentham to be indebted to a man he didn't trust. He had no doubt

Seymour had his price. The fact that he was still trying to encourage him to take an interest in his daughter suggested the man was not too particular in his morals. As long as Trentham married his daughter, Seymour would not have cared if all Louisa's stories had been true.

His eye fell irresistibly on Eleanor Seymour again. She was pretty enough, he supposed, but far too young, besides which, it had not escaped his attention that Mr Burnley was rarely far from her side. No doubt tonight's little charade had been intended to make Mr Burnley jealous. Judging from the way the older man was glowering, she had been only too successful.

Even so, Trentham could not help remembering their first meeting. He had danced with her at a ball once, before he knew who she was. He had even been quite taken with her, until one of his friends had drawn him aside.

'Be careful of that little filly. You know who her father is, don't you?'

'Someone by the name of Seymour, I presume,' he replied dryly.

'Have you never heard of Mrs Gregory's lapdog? He'll stop at nothing to make a good match for the girl and will then spend the rest of his life bleeding his son-in-law dry.'

And sure enough, only a few days afterwards, he had heard the first of many rumours about Miss Eleanor Seymour's marriage prospects. To be so talked about and still neither married nor engaged was not a good thing. He only hoped for the girl's sake nothing would go wrong with Mr Burnley. If that match fell through, no-one would want to touch her with a barge pole.

* * *

Eleanor watched the light creep across her narrow room, illuminating the old-fashioned furniture, which was not quite good enough for the main bedrooms. Her room faced east, so she was always awake at dawn, no matter how late it was when she finally got to bed. Her window overlooked a court-yard of outbuildings. Footsteps rang on the paved yard, intermingled with the voices of the servants.

Initially, she had loitered in her room, musing about the events of the previous day or trying to read until the rest of the household was up. But after she had been at Deepwater for a week, she made a sudden resolution. Surely no-one could have any objection if she got up and went out into the garden for a breath of air.

She had not gone far, however, when a ball bounced round the corner of the house. It was followed by a spaniel puppy, whose feet and ears seemed far too large for the rest of its body, and a little figure with tumbling curls and a white gown, her sash half-untied.

The puppy was the first to notice Eleanor. It stopped abruptly, braced its stumpy legs and began to growl. The little girl, not anticipating this sudden halt, barely avoided tripping over her pet. Two pairs of large, brown eyes turned to survey Eleanor.

'I didn't mean to frighten you. I'm Miss Seymour, one of Mr Trentham's guests,' Eleanor explained.

'How do you do?'

The little girl dropped a curtsey. Then her irrepressible nature burst through the polite rituals that had been drilled into her.

'Mr Trentham is my guardian,' she announced with considerable pride.

They were startled by a woman's voice.

'Mary! Mary, you naughty child, where are you?'

Mary bit her lip and smiled apologetically. The puppy, deciding Eleanor was not dangerous, sniffed the hem of her dress, then bounded away to pounce on the forgotten ball. Mary's nurse panted into sight.

'There you are, child. Will you look at the mess you're — oh, I beg your pardon. I didn't know there was anyone about.'

'It really doesn't matter.'

Mary glanced ruefully at the dangling ends of her sash.

'I didn't mean to be naughty,' she said beseechingly. 'It was Frisk that ran away. I was only trying to catch him. You know how cross the gardener was when he dug up the flowerbeds, yesterday.'

'Aye, well.' The maid rumpled her apron unconsciously. 'We'll talk about that later.'

'Frisk is my puppy,' Mary exclaimed, turning her bright face towards Eleanor. 'He's only six months old. My guardian gave him to me.'

'That was kind of him,' Eleanor said. She could see there was a strong resemblance between Mr Trentham and the child, except in the colour of their eyes.

'Yes, but he says I won't be able to take Frisk with me when I go to school,' Mary persisted. 'He says the mistresses won't allow it, not even if I asked them very nicely.'

'He's probably right.'

Eleanor was struggling to adapt her opinion of Trentham and the effort was making her dizzy. She had imagined he would be aloof, whereas it was clear the little girl could talk to him freely.

'Don't you like the idea of going to school?'

Mary tilted her head to one side.

'I want to go to school,' she announced, 'but I want to stay here, too. I like the garden and Frisk and my room, but there isn't anyone to play with. I think that's why Mr Trentham gave me Frisk.'

There was a lot more Eleanor would have liked to ask her, but Frisk came lolloping along at that moment, ball clamped between his teeth.

'Then perhaps you had better go and play with him,' Eleanor suggested.

Mary began to run, then remembering her manners, stopped, bobbed another curtsey and dashed off again with the nurse.

Eleanor watched them go. Mary was not at all what she had expected. She had thought she would be a thoughtful, timid child, pining for her absent mother or cowed by her guardian, unaware he was really her father.

* * *

'I think I should like to sit down for a while,' Mrs Gregory remarked.

Eleanor could not help feeling disappointed, but obediently she turned back. The weather was much too beautiful to stay indoors and they had only been strolling about the garden for half an hour. As they turned the last corner, they caught sight of an unfamiliar vehicle outside the front door. Its seat was set high above four wheels and the pair of grey horses was so well matched, they might almost have been twins.

The front door opened and Eleanor turned to see Trentham coming down the steps, clad in his riding coat of bottle-green and carrying a pair of buff gloves. He had a preoccupied air, which

Mrs Gregory didn't seem to notice.

'Ah, Trentham,' she said. 'I take it this is your monstrosity.'

He bowed slightly.

'It is at your service whenever you wish,' he said, drawing on his gloves.

'Oh, no, I wouldn't dream of risking my life in that thing. At my age, you find, young man, that every day is precious.'

Eleanor, used to being ignored, was unprepared for what Mrs Gregory said next.

'But Miss Seymour was saying she would like a ride in a phaeton.'

She was blatantly fishing for an invitation, or that was what Trentham would think.

'Oh, no, madam, I never said that,' she gasped, but her voice was drowned out by Mrs Gregory's.

'You are not going anywhere in particular, are you?'

'Only to settle a dispute between two of my tenants,' he replied dryly.

The older woman seemed oblivious

to the ironic edge in his voice.

'Then you'll have no objection to taking Miss Seymour with you.'

She turned and smiled genially at Eleanor, saying, 'There you are, child. Your wish will be granted.'

'But I cannot put Mr Trentham to so much trouble.'

'No trouble at all. That thing seats two quite comfortably, doesn't it?'

Trentham nodded, cocking his eyebrow at Eleanor.

'Don't tell me after all your brave words you are frightened, Miss Seymour, or don't you trust Mr Trentham's driving?'

'It's not that,' Eleanor blundered.

'Well, then, that's settled.'

Eleanor exchanged glances with Trentham. There was no getting out of it. Mrs Gregory was waiting on the doorstep to make sure Eleanor made good her boast. Trentham offered her his hand to help her ascent. It was even higher from above than it appeared from the ground and she felt a moment's dizziness as she settled herself in the seat beside Trentham.

Even before they set off, the phaeton seemed to sway with their every movement. She felt terribly exposed, visible for miles around and apparently coupled with Trentham. He waved his hat to Mrs Gregory and they set off at an energetic pace, causing Eleanor to hold tight to the seat with one hand and snatch at her broad-brimmed hat with the other.

As soon as they turned the first curve in the drive, she nerved herself to speak to the gentleman beside her.

'I really am dreadfully sorry,' she said, brushing a stray ringlet away from her mouth. 'Perhaps you could set me down somewhere. I didn't mean to be a nuisance.'

A flash of amusement flickered in his eye.

'And what would you say to Mrs Gregory if she saw you returning alone?'

Eleanor never completed her reply. The phaeton suddenly jolted and skittered to a standstill, just outside the gates. She had taken her eyes off the road for a moment, but thankfully Trentham had not. A woman in black had appeared from between the trees and was standing motionless on the dusty road, barely a foot away from the horses' heads.

5

'You might have been killed,' he gasped, gazing stonily at the woman standing there defiantly.

Eleanor felt her blood run cold as the stranger fixed her dark eyes on Trentham's face. It was the same woman who had stabbed him at Vauxhall.

'Oh, no, I know you better than that, James,' she said. 'I know how skilled you are, to a fraction of an inch.'

She made no attempt to move. The road was narrow and passing her would have meant driving partly along the grassy verge between the road and a drainage ditch.

'I thought I told you I never wished to lay eyes on you again.'

She came forward and ran her fingers down the muzzle of the nearest horse.

'Oh, but you didn't mean that, just as

I didn't mean for that other incident to happen in London. We were both angry, but you said you forgave me for that.'

'I forgive you,' Trentham muttered through gritted teeth.

He threw an uneasy glance at Eleanor. It seemed to alert the stranger to the fact they were not alone.

'Has he deceived you, too?' she asked, looking Eleanor up and down as if she were a curious specimen. 'No, I don't suppose he has, since you are still sitting by his side. But you shouldn't believe his professions of love, you know. He will always love me best.'

'Miss Alcock!' Trentham exploded.

'You always called me Louisa before,' she flashed back. 'I won't answer to any other name.'

'Miss Alcock, be reasonable.'

Trentham's unease was palpable. Eleanor wanted to intervene, but was afraid of making things worse. She didn't know which side to take. She didn't like Trentham much, but the incident at Vauxhall was still vivid in her memory. Louisa Alcock covered both ears with her hands and went on inexorably, this time directing her gaze at Eleanor.

'Did he tell you how we met? It is such a romantic story. We knew from the very first moment . . .'

'Louisa, be quiet!'

She stopped abruptly and stretched out her hand to the horse's head again, but she was no longer stroking it. Instead her fingers curled round the leather strap that crossed its cheek. She smiled provocatively, as if asking him what he intended to do next.

Trentham hesitated, glancing first at Eleanor, then at the horses.

'Do you think you could manage to hold this pair steady?' he asked. 'They're rather high-spirited.'

'I'll do my best.'

Eleanor heard her voice quaver, in spite of her efforts to control it.

'Not good enough,' he muttered. 'You must be firm and not allow them to get the upper hand of you.'

That, Eleanor mused, had been her trouble all her life. She had never stood her ground firmly enough. Even so, Trentham handed the reins over to her, made sure she was holding them properly and jumped down.

'Wait for me here.'

Louisa Alcock released the horse and moved aside, out of earshot, though her eyes remained fixed on the phaeton. Suddenly afraid, Eleanor breathed, 'Are you sure this is wise?'

He replied only with a look. Snatching Louisa by the arm none too gently, he dragged her some distance away from the phaeton. Eleanor was caught between curiosity and the feeling that this was none of her business.

Trentham and the stranger spoke in angry whispers. Eleanor shifted uneasily. If Louisa Alcock attacked him again, what should she do?

There was no sign of a knife, however. Trentham bent his head closer to hers, while Louisa held him tightly

78

by the sleeves. Eleanor saw one hand slide caressingly along his arm from elbow to shoulder and back again. Louisa seemed to be talking in a continuous babble, interrupted now and then by a curt interjection from Trentham. Only the occasional word or phrase was loud enough for Eleanor to make it out.

'No!' she heard, then again, 'No, no, it's unthinkable,' and in a softer tone, 'Why won't you understand?'

Eleanor shivered. Louisa's voice was taking on a trembling cadence, as if she were about to cry. What had Trentham done to this woman to reduce her to begging for his favour?

'No, James, don't!' Louisa cried out as he wrenched himself free. 'You can't leave me like this. You cannot deny the truth. James, have pity on me.'

She ran after him and, as he leaped into the seat of the phaeton, she caught the skirts of his coat.

'For goodness' sake, leave me alone!' he bellowed, raising his arm as if to strike her.

Eleanor gasped, too shocked to have the presence of mind to snatch his sleeve, but Louisa didn't even flinch. Her huge brown eyes continued gazing up at him, luminous with unshed tears.

'I knew you couldn't do it,' she said. 'Doesn't that show you how much you still care for me?'

Trentham lowered his arm with a moan.

'Why do you insist on tormenting us both like this?'

'It will all be over soon, one way or another,' she whispered. 'I promise you that.'

Whether in response to some signal from their master or from uneasiness, the horses shifted forward a pace or two. As Trentham saw she was clear of the back wheel, he lashed the horses into a gallop.

Louisa ran after them as long as she could, crying out, begging. Eleanor couldn't help glancing over her shoulder. She saw Louisa come to a standstill in the middle of the road, her arms stretched towards them, tears streaming down her cheeks.

'Please, stop. We cannot leave her like that.'

Trentham kept his eyes on the road. He paid no heed to her attempts to persuade him to slow down. For perhaps half a mile, they charged on, swaying dangerously round bends in the road. Luckily they met no one along the way. When he did at last slow their pace, it seemed more to spare the horses than because he was aware he was endangering himself and his passenger. He didn't speak immediately and nor did Eleanor. It was obvious Louisa was his cast-off love but unlike other mistresses, Louisa would not go quietly when she was dismissed. Moreover, Eleanor was shocked Trentham could even threaten violence against a woman he had already injured. And this was the man on whose whim her safety depended until she could escape from the phaeton.

Trentham turned on her with a fierce scowl.

'I suppose you presume to judge me on the strength of what you have just witnessed,' he demanded.

'It's none of my business,' she retorted primly.

'No, that's right, nor anyone else's for that matter. But that doesn't usually prevent people from talking.'

'Now you are judging me.'

'Let's not waste any more time, Miss Seymour. What price do you ask for your silence?'

She stared at him aghast, unable to utter a word. He wanted to buy her off! He thought she could be paid to forget what she had seen. Her pride and her sense of honour were wounded.

'Well, well, come along. I haven't got all day.'

'I don't want your money.'

'So what do you want? Clothes? Jewels? A sinecure for your father? A proposal of marriage?'

Eleanor was stung by the sneer in his voice.

'I don't want anything from you. You cannot buy me.'

'So you intend to tell the whole world what you saw.'

'Let me out. I'll walk back to the hall.'

She couldn't bear to be so close to him for a second longer. This was the brutal, ugly face of wealth. He thought he could betray one woman with impunity and bribe another into preserving his precious reputation.

'Did you hear what I said? Let me out.'

In reply, Trentham urged his horses faster.

'You cannot keep me in this phaeton for ever.'

'I'm well aware of that, but I won't leave you until I know you are in a safe place.'

'What harm can befall me on a quiet country lane? Are you afraid of footpads or highwaymen?'

Trentham glanced at her briefly.

'You might meet Miss Alcock along the way.'

Eleanor smiled wryly.

'Are you really so afraid of what she might tell me about your shameful past?'

The horses stopped suddenly.

'No, damn you, I am afraid she might kill you. Wasn't her behaviour at Vauxhall a sufficient demonstration to you what she is capable of?'

Eleanor forced herself to laugh incredulously, but the scene flashed before her eyes. The knife broken against a metal button, the blood seeping through his shirt, the gash that might have been much more severe if fate had not intervened. The fear she had felt for her father when he had gone after that woman.

'Why should she want to kill me?' she asked.

'Because she believes you are her rival for my affections.'

Eleanor was silenced. To her knowledge, Louisa had seen her three times in apparently intimate contact with Trentham. Something about his tone convinced her that he believed what he was saying.

'But if she is so dangerous, why is she allowed to roam free? Why didn't you want her to be arrested in London?'

'Your father didn't tell you all about her?'

'No.'

Trentham digested this news in silence. Eleanor felt a little flare of triumph. For once, her father had been more trustworthy than most people gave him credit for. Maybe Trentham would think twice before he abused her family again. He threw her an evaluating look, trying to decide if she could be trusted.

'It will have to wait till later,' he said. 'This business is more urgent.'

They had reached their destination. He fastened his horses to an iron ring in the wall outside a farmhouse before helping Eleanor out. She was surprised how much her legs quivered. Without ceremony, Trentham turned her over to the farmer's wife, who seemed only too pleased to show Eleanor her chickens, dairy and vegetable garden.

Her mind was so full, she could only reply in monosyllables. Eventually she became aware the farmer's wife was praising Mr Trentham as a landlord, because he always took an interest in the land and, unlike some other landowners she could name, he had not pressed them for rent when the crops failed several years ago. It did not strike her till later the reason why she had been told all this was because the farmer's wife assumed Mr Trentham was courting her.

The return journey was strained. For a long while neither of them spoke.

'I would appreciate it if you told nobody about what you have seen or heard today,' Trentham said tonelessly, staring straight ahead of him.

'If you had had the courtesy to ask me sooner instead of trying to buy me off, no power on earth could make me reveal your secrets.'

Eleanor knew in her heart of hearts she would do as he asked, but it wouldn't do him any harm to be kept on tenterhooks.

'I suppose you think I ought to marry her,' he growled.

'I don't think anything about it at all,' Eleanor replied as sweetly as possible.

'Her family believes it is the only way to cure her infatuation, and never mind the consequences.'

'It would have been wise to think about the consequences before you seduced her.'

Trentham laughed bitterly.

'Is that what you think happened? I never did anything to encourage the girl, except be kind to her. The romantic way in which we met — I pulled her out of a river after she half-drowned during a silly prank. When I realised she was becoming infatuated, I tried to distance myself from her as gently as I could, but she refused to understand.'

'Do you really expect me to believe that? Miss Alcock is very beautiful. I should have thought any man would be flattered to earn her admiration.'

'I admit my vanity was piqued at first. But . . . ' He broke off suddenly, as if remembering to whom he was talking.

'But?' Eleanor prompted.

'I'd rather not speak about it.'

They had come so far, Eleanor was not prepared to let the matter drop that easily.

'If you are innocent, why all the secrecy?'

'Not for my sake, I assure you. You may say what you please about me. But the Alcocks are a respectable family. I hoped to spare them public embarrassment. Louisa, too, if she ever recovers from this madness, which I am beginning to doubt.'

'She seemed sane enough to me,' Eleanor lied.

'Did she? Is a woman who writes letters declaring her devotion three or

88

four times a day sane? She follows me wherever I go, she tells complete strangers that we are betrothed or that I have never loved anyone but her. You saw what she did in Vauxhall.'

'What about Mary, or is she the daughter of one of your other mistresses?'

'This has nothing to do with Mary.'

His fierceness made Eleanor flinch. He was physically so close, she could feel his muscles tense as they approached the stretch of road where they had met Louisa, but there was nobody about. Trentham let out a deep breath as they turned into the drive.

In the week that followed, there was stalemate between Eleanor and Trentham. He spent more time in her company, and she realised he was watching her, waiting for her to make a move. He never said much to her directly, but she knew he didn't trust her.

It was hard to behave naturally and she drew deeper into her shell. She wavered between wanting to prove him wrong and the urge to do something rash. He thought the worst of her anyway. What difference would it make if she did tell Harriet about Louisa?

She met Mary several times in the garden, taking Frisk for a run before the sun grew too hot. Eleanor made a habit of her early morning walks, since that was the only time of day she could be sure of avoiding Mr Burnley.

But she was puzzled. If Louisa was not Mary's mother, who was? And why should Trentham deny that, when he had admitted so much else to her?

When she mentioned Mary to Mrs Gregory, she was swamped by a stream of praise for Trentham's generosity in taking her in.

'Surely that is the least he can do for his own daughter?' Eleanor suggested.

'His? Who told you that?' Mrs Gregory went on before Eleanor could reply, 'No, Mary is a legacy from his brother. Got himself killed in a duel after a drunken quarrel.'

She launched into a long story, leaving Eleanor in a quandary. If Trentham had been telling the truth about Mary, should she believe what he said about Louisa?

★　★　★

As Trentham made his way towards his dancing partner, he noticed the Seymour girl sitting on the edge of the room. As far as he could tell, she had not yet spread any rumours about him. He had been very alert over the past days, but he could detect no change in the behaviour of his guests.

The real test would be tonight, at the grand ball he was holding. If she were intent on damaging him, she would choose this night of all nights to do it. As well as his house guests, most of his neighbours would be there. Gossip would spread like wildfire.

The drawing-room had been almost cleared of furniture to allow room for dancing. There were several card tables set up in the library and supper would be served later in the dining-room.

He forced himself to concentrate. As the host, he was expected to open the ball with a minuet with the daughter of the local Member of Parliament. He didn't intend to dance much after that. He had other duties to attend to.

Once the minuet was over, he found himself watching Eleanor Seymour again, wondering who her first partner would be. Mr Burnley was by her side as usual. A flame of irritation shot through Trentham. One thing he had learned from watching her was that she was intelligent, too intelligent to throw herself away on someone like Mr Burnley. She never said much, but he had the impression that very little escaped her. That was what made her a dangerous enemy, if she was an enemy. At times she seemed so vulnerable.

As Trentham passed her on his way to greet a late arrival, she glanced up, her eyes pleading, but her expression changed when she saw who he was.

That look stung his conscience. He could see her stay in his house had not hitherto been a happy one. The set began to form for the first country dance and he realised no-one had asked Miss Seymour to dance. He acted on impulse. Before he was aware of what he was doing, he was by her side.

'Are you engaged for the next dance, Miss Seymour?'

6

Her lashes swept upwards and she could not conceal the astonishment in her eyes. Then her mouth hardened and she raised her chin proudly.

'No, sir, not yet.'

Was she annoyed with him for interrupting her tête-à-tête, or was she embarrassed because he had noticed that no-one had asked her? Having gone this far, he could not back down, but it was with some reluctance that he asked his next question.

'Would you care to dance with me, then?'

She glanced at Mr Burnley before she placed her hand in his.

'Thank you, you are very kind, sir,' she said, as if she wished he was at the devil.

His mood was by no means improved when he noticed how many eyes followed them to the set. Whispers rustled behind fluttering fans. For such an eligible bachelor to dance with the MP's daughter was perfectly natural. That his second choice should be a fortune hunter barely tolerated by Society, when so many respectable girls were pining for a partner, was not quite a scandal, but very near it.

They exchanged only a few terse remarks before the music began. Miss Seymour seemed visibly relieved that, with the complicated sequence of crossing and turning, conversation was impossible. The tune was a lively one and in spite of himself, Trentham began to be infected by its mood.

Glancing across the set at his partner, he saw that her eyes had begun to sparkle. A smile tugged at her lips and her cheeks had grown flushed with exertion. From being merely pretty, she had become almost beautiful. They reached the bottom of the set and had to stand out during one repetition of the dance before they could join in again. Conversation of some sort was necessary. She looked up into his face and her smile faded.

It was the first time they had been alone since the incident in the phaeton. He suddenly remembered how different it had been the first time he had danced with her. She had seemed sweet and shy back then and utterly unspoiled. Had he misjudged her?

'I hope you are enjoying your stay in Nottinghamshire,' he said, for want of anything better to say, and then realised how stupid the remark was, knowing what he knew about this girl.

'Yes, thank you,' she replied heavily. With a sudden resolution she added, 'I would enjoy myself a great deal more if I felt you trusted me.'

The colour crept into his cheeks.

'We seem to have set out on the wrong footing,' he admitted. 'I am sorry you have been obliged to scold me about my bad manners yet again.'

Unexpectedly, she smiled. The transformation was magical. The careworn look disappeared from her face and she looked as beautiful as she had while she was dancing. A nagging voice in his head warned him it was a trap to ensnare him, but he ignored it.

'I didn't mean to scold . . . ' she began, but the time had come for them to resume dancing.

Now that the air had been cleared, Trentham enjoyed the dance even more than before. Eleanor Seymour was quick and graceful. She had no trouble remembering the figures of the dance and he was almost sorry when they reached the top of the set and had to stand out again.

'May I ask you something?' she asked hesitantly.

'Certainly.'

'Why didn't you tell me Mary was your niece?'

'Mary's mother is a married woman now. Her husband is in the navy and doesn't know Mary exists.'

She obviously felt uncomfortable about prying. She glanced nervously over her shoulder. True to his character, Mr Burnley was still in the same chair, feet planted wide apart and one hand resting on each knee. The Seymour girl shivered and before he had a chance to think, Trentham blurted out, 'Has Mr Burnley been boring you with his talk?'

She darted up a confused look.

'No,' she lied, unconvincingly.

'You should think long and hard, Miss Seymour, before you unite yourself with a man who annoys you even before you are obliged to humour his whims, day and night.'

Her chin shot up again and her eyes sparkled.

'I shall bear your advice in mind,' she retorted haughtily. 'I assume that is why you are still a bachelor. You couldn't find anyone willing to indulge your moods?'

As she flung herself back into the dance, Trentham bit his lip. Why did he have to complicate matters, when everything had been going so well?

His duties as host kept him occupied

after the dance was over and he lost sight of Miss Seymour until he saw her at supper, attended once more by Mr Burnley. So much for heeding his advice. She was a hopeless case and he must stop thinking about her.

Later, back home, Eleanor listened to the steps as they came upstairs. She had undressed, with Dinah's assistance, but she knew there was no hope of sleep for her that night.

Dancing with Mr Trentham had been a welcome interlude. She almost despised herself for feeling so grateful to him for helping her to escape from Mr Burnley. Her elderly admirer had pursued her doggedly all evening, making remarks about the sanctity of marriage.

She had hoped her father might drop a few gentle hints to Mr Burnley before things went too far. But when she asked to speak to him, Mr Seymour brushed her off with, 'Later, Eleanor. Can't you see I'm busy?'

Dancing had only been a brief respite. Mr Burnley had hunted her down as soon as she was without a partner in order to compliment her on the fleetness of her foot.

'Such an innocent diversion,' he went on. 'I'm sure a little gentle exercise must do everyone good. It has put a pretty colour in your cheeks and a twinkle in your eye.'

Flattery always made her feel awkward, but Mr Burnley was not to be deterred. When she tried deflecting him on to other topics, he praised her for her modesty. He stuck by her during supper then kept an iron grip on her hand as he steered her to the most secluded part of the drawing-room.

'We won't be interrupted here,' he smirked at her. 'I have something of the utmost importance to say to you. The fact is, Miss Seymour, you have captivated my heart.'

'Mr Burnley!'

He ignored the interruption.

'No, let me finish. I wish to lay my fortune at your dainty, little feet. You may do what you like with it, if only you agree to marry me.'

I don't want your money, her heart screamed. But her head knew that they needed it. Eleanor was realistic enough to see there were no other candidates. But when she looked at Mr Burnley, she acted on impulse.

'I am flattered, of course, sir, but I cannot possibly marry you. The disparity in our ages and fortunes is so great.'

'I am willing to overlook your lack of dowry. I'll settle money on you. You will be a rich widow, quite independent of everyone. I'll take care of your father's debts.'

'You cannot buy me!'

She dug her nails into his hand and, with a yelp of pain and surprise, he released her. All her wildcat instincts roused at last, Eleanor did not care what methods she used to get free. She would bite if she needed to. Mr Burnley's expression changed. His cheeks became mottled with red, his eyebrows drew together.

'What do you mean by this? Your

father told me you were willing.'

'He had no right to. I am of age and can do as I please.'

This was visibly a shock to Mr Burnley. Eleanor bit her lips. She should not have said that. It was placing a weapon in the hands of someone who would pretty soon be an open enemy. She had lashed out solely because it was a blow to discover her father had condoned this match behind her back.

She guessed that, to salve his hurt pride, Mr Burnley would tell himself he was lucky to have seen her vixenish temper before he made the mistake of marrying her. Whether he would say that to other people depended on whether he thought revenge was adequate compensation for being laughed at for making a fool of himself over her.

'You can't do anything without money,' he began again.

'I can earn it like other people do.'

'I know what this really means,' he said. 'Don't expect Trentham to marry you, because he won't.'

Eleanor pretended not to hear. She fled into the hall before she said something she would regret. Her father would think she had inflicted enough damage on the family as it was.

A sudden rustling, like mice under the floorboards, made her look up sharply and raise her candle. There was a little white figure on the stairs. Eleanor could not see her face, but by her size, it could only be Mary.

'What are you doing here?' Eleanor called.

'Oh, it's you,' Mary said with a sigh of relief and came two steps farther down. 'I only wanted to hear the music and see the pretty ladies.'

'It's very late.'

'I know. My nurse is asleep, but I just couldn't sleep. It's too exciting.'

Eleanor suddenly felt very tired, and yet the prospect of being locked in her room with only her thoughts for company was not appealing. She sat down on a step and Mary scrambled down to snuggle against her. She was shivering, with cold or excitement.

'I got lonely up there,' Mary explained.

'I know. I'm often lonely, too, and then I wish my mother was still alive.'

'Is your mamma dead?' Mary asked, looking up at her with huge eyes.

'Yes. What about you?'

The little girl considered this matter for a moment as she rested her tumbled head against Eleanor's shoulder.

'No, she's not dead, she just can't take care of me, Mr Trentham says.'

Eleanor was not sure if this was a good idea or not. But perhaps this way finding out the truth when she was older would not be so hard for her.

'You must miss her.'

'Yes,' she drawled, playing with her fingers. 'I used to wish I was like other girls and made up stories about her. But it's much better here than the place I was before. The nurse there was often cross with me. Mr Trentham is never angry, or hardly ever, only when I've been really, really naughty.'

I think Mr Trentham is cross with me at the moment, Eleanor thought, but she did not speak the worlds aloud. It was all very well for him to tell her to keep away from Mr Burnley, but what was she supposed to do now? And what would her father say?

'I wish you were my mother,' Mary murmured sleepily.

'Well, young lady, what explanation do you have for this misdemeanor?'

A voice beneath them in the hall made them both jump. Trentham fixed them with a steady gaze.

'I don't know what that means — that last word.'

'Can't you guess?'

'She only wanted to listen to the music,' Eleanor intervened, scrambling to her feet. 'I'll see she goes back to bed.'

'Make sure she does. It's far too late for a child to be up.'

Eleanor bobbed her head slightly and tried to guide the little girl upstairs.

Mary broke free, however, and ran down the steps, stopping Mr Trentham in his tracks.

'You're not angry with me, are you, sir?'

'No. Not much at any rate.'

The little imp grinned and held out her arms.

'Then why didn't you give me my good-night kiss?'

Trentham threw a self-conscious look at Eleanor, who pretended to be busy inspecting the banisters, though she couldn't suppress a smile.

'Oh, very well, little monkey!'

He lifted her off her feet so suddenly that Mary squealed with pleasure. He allowed her to cling round his neck for a moment and planted a kiss on her cheek, before he put her down again.

'Now run along. I shall ask Miss Seymour if you behaved yourself and, mark my words, if she makes the slightest complaint about you, there'll be trouble.'

With another suppressed squeal, Mary bounded up the stairs and squeezed Eleanor's hand. She sighed as the door shut behind her guardian.

'Isn't he the nicest, handsomest, bestest man in the world?' she asked.

Eleanor lay awake the best part of that night, drowsing fitfully now and then. She woke at dawn, feeling as if her head was full of stinging nettles, but so awake, she knew she wouldn't be able to sleep again.

She could near noises in the yard and got up to peep outside. The sun, sitting on the silvery slate roof opposite her, dazzled her. Shielding her eyes with her hand, she made out a boy cleaning shoes in the courtyard and a maid hurrying towards the dairy. The hazy sky suggested the promise of a lovely summer's day. If the servants were up, some of the doors must be unlocked. Perhaps a walk would make her sleepy and she would be able to have a nap before breakfast.

She managed to dress herself without calling Dinah, but it took much longer than she expected. Tiredness made her more clumsy and prone to tears than usual. She crept along the landing in her stockinged feet, carrying her much-mended shoes. The heel of one of her stockings was darned, as was the toe of the other. She hoped she wouldn't meet anyone along the way. No-one stirred.

At the foot of the stairs she met with a disappointment. The front door was still barred and chained. Her only hope now was either the kitchen door, into the courtyard beneath her bedroom, or a little side door next to the dining-room. She sat down to put on her shoes and trod as softly as she could. In the drawing-room and dining-room, the servants were bustling about, sweeping the floors, removing dead flowers, scraping off spilt candle wax and polishing every surface until it shone.

Eleanor passed by unmolested. It seemed too much to hope for, but the side door yielded beneath her hand and she found herself breathing in the fresh, dew-drenched air. She was on a narrow, gravel path between shrubs, which led out into a sunny lawn, glistening with a thousand diamonds. Ignoring Mrs Gregory's advice never to get her feet wet, she cut across the grass, leaving a dark green trail behind her in the dew.

All around her she could hear birds singing. They swished past her, beaks full of worms or flies for their second brood of fledglings. She had missed all this in London. In spite of all she had to worry her, Eleanor felt soothed.

There was an artificial lake at the far end of the garden. A path led all the way around it, with trees and shrubs to provide shade in summer. On one of the banks there was a little summer-house. Perhaps she could sit there for a while and admire the view. She picked up a quicker pace and, as she turned a bend, she came face to face with Mr Trentham.

He was wearing nothing but a pair of breeches. A towel only half-concealed his broad chest and the smooth muscles in his shoulders. His hair was wet and droplets of water stood out on his naked torso and the livid scar along his breastbone.

7

Eleanor knew she ought not look, but there was a strange fascination in the sight. He was trembling barely perceptibly in the cool air.

'I — I'm sorry,' she stammered, backing away.

She tried looking at his face, but he seemed embarrassed at being caught like this, so she dropped her eyes again.

'There is no need to apologise. You took me by surprise,' he replied.

Momentarily Eleanor smiled up into his face and this time prudently averted her eyes. There was something disturbing about encountering such a sight so early in the morning, when she had believed herself to be alone in the garden. Her glance fell on the steps leading into the summerhouse. He had dropped his shirt there in a careless tangle, as if he had been too impatient for his swim to fold it.

'I couldn't sleep,' she excused herself.

'Neither could I,' and on a sudden impulse, Trentham added, 'I often swim here in summer, every day if I have the opportunity.'

He stooped to retrieve his shirt with a rueful smile.

'I'd better go,' she said, tearing her eyes away from him.

'Don't let me disturb your walk. You must feel free to come and go as you please.'

'Thank you.'

'Mary didn't cause you any trouble last night, did she?'

'No, I managed to tuck her in without waking her nurse.'

'Until breakfast, then?'

He seemed almost determined to keep her there, though he had not yet put on his shirt.

'Yes, sir. Good-day, sir.'

'Good day, Miss Seymour.'

Even without the meeting by the lake, James Trentham thought he would

112

have noticed Eleanor Seymour at breakfast. For one thing, only a small, hardy group was up yet. Many of the others had chosen to have breakfast in bed, or were still asleep, nursing throbbing heads.

But after the curiously intimate scene in the garden, he found himself gazing at her. He had felt at a disadvantage, dishevelled and wet, when she appeared, looking trim and neat, despite the fact the jacket and petticoat of her walking-dress had faded from vivid blue to grey. A more coquettish girl might have teased him; a vengeful one would have kept him talking, while the cold seeped deeper and deeper into his bones.

What made the situation worse was that he had been thinking about her all night. He dreamed he was dancing with her and she rose on tiptoe and brushed her lips against his. The kiss woke him, bewildered, outraged, yet infinitely happy. Unable to understand the absurd dream, he had gone into the garden, hoping a cold dip might clear his head.

It had taken him longer than usual to tire himself, but he was just congratulating himself on the success of his stratagem when there she was before him, her eyes as restless as if she had really kissed him the previous night. She was quiet now. A shaft of light caught her face, revealing how pale and heavy-eyed she was and he wondered what had kept her awake. He hardly thought it could be the excitement of the ball. Perhaps she had been planning her wedding to Mr Burnley.

The notion was more repugnant than ever this morning. He sipped his coffee, but he couldn't get rid of the bitter taste in his mouth. Mr Burnley looked more solemn than usual and Trentham noticed that Seymour's attempts to humour him went unheeded.

He saw the two men disappear into the garden after breakfast. Eleanor watched them pass the drawing-room window, her hands clenched so tightly, her knuckles turned white. He had no doubt she knew what her father and suitor intended to discuss. Trentham could have made a fair guess at it himself. He had a dozen letters to write but, perversely, he dropped into an armchair next to Mrs Gregory. Eleanor Seymour sat beside her, sewing diligently. He wanted to observe her. The letters could wait.

'You agree with me, don't you, Mr Trentham?' Mrs Gregory asked.

'I beg your pardon? I'm afraid I wasn't attending,' he murmured, ashamed at being caught daydreaming.

'You agree that prudent matches are necessary for the good of Society.'

A sudden surge of emotion overwhelmed him. He had heard enough talk of weddings, marriage settlements and money recently to last him a lifetime.

'Certainly, but there is a vast difference between a prudent match and a mercenary one.'

If he could make Eleanor squirm, there might be a chance of saving her.

She rose to the bait.

'What should a woman do if her parents forbid her to marry the man she loves, because he is too poor? Is she to blame for the sort of match she makes?'

She choked and Trentham saw the glitter of tears on her lashes. Her words suggested a past history he had no business to pry into. She had been disappointed in love and now, to revenge herself on the world, she would marry a rich, old man, only to discover she was punishing herself instead. He had seen it happen before. The feverish search for diversion, filling the drawing-room with guests, so she wouldn't have to be alone with her husband, the scandal of a dalliance with a younger man.

'So you would prefer love in a cottage to wealth without esteem?' he persisted.

'Some of us have no choice in the matter.'

The bleakness of this statement moved him unexpectedly. But Mrs Gregory intervened.

'Nonsense. There is always a choice.

If nothing else, you can choose to submit to your fate gracefully.'

The door opened and Eleanor flinched at the sight of her father. For a moment, Mr Seymour, too, looked uncharacteristically grave. His ingratiating smile returned when Mrs Gregory accosted him.

'Ah, Seymour, did you know your daughter was a rebel?'

Eleanor drew in her breath. Clearly she knew a storm was about to break over her head. Trentham searched frantically for a way to change the subject.

'Speaking of which, have you read the latest news from America?' he asked.

The look Seymour threw at Eleanor was not lost on Trentham. He would bide his time, but sooner or later, he would speak to his daughter alone. Perhaps by evening, the engagement would be announced, or would it be more in Seymour's style to entrust it as a great secret to each of the principal gossips in the house so the news would spread as inexorably as ivy creeping up a wall?

★ ★ ★

'Eleanor, do you know what you have done?'

'I believe so, Papa.'

The endearment did not soften his temper. Eleanor had witnessed many of his outbursts, but she knew this might be far worse than any of the others. Her only chance lay in the fact they were in the garden and liable to be overheard.

'Do you really? Are you aware of how much money I owe Burnley? That very dress on your back was paid for out of a loan he gave me.'

She flushed. She had assumed the sums of money her father had flashed around before they left London had come from Trentham.

'I was under the impression this gown had not been paid for at all.'

'Don't be flippant, madam,' Mr

118

Seymour growled. 'Thank goodness I persuaded him this was just a girlish trick to whet his appetite.'

Eleanor groped for words, but her father went on.

'Do you have any idea what might happen if I let Mr Burnley go back to London in his current frame of mind? Our credit would be shot to pieces. We could never set foot in town again without the danger of being arrested.'

'But you cannot expect me to marry him.'

'I know it is not the sort of marriage a girl would usually welcome, but what other choice do we have?'

This was the first hint Eleanor had seen of her father's true feelings. If he, too, was not set upon this match, she might be able to sway him.

'There must be some other way to extricate ourselves from this mountain of debt.'

'Oh, indeed? Perhaps I ought to turn over all my account books, bills and dunning letters to you?'

Perhaps you should! I could hardly make a worse hash of them than you have. The words were on her lips, but she bit them back. Antagonising her father would only make things worse.

Grudgingly, he softened his tone.

'All I ask for the present, Nell, is that you flirt with Burnley a little. Make sure he doesn't leave before you have put him in a better temper. Then at the end of our stay here, if you don't find anyone who is willing to marry you, we'll talk about the matter again.'

It was unlike her father to be so conciliatory. Was it only because he was not in his own home, or did he have another motive? His words were a challenge. *If you can't find a husband yourself, you'll have to accept my choice.* For a split second, the encounter by the lake dashed across her vision. And then she heard Mr Burnley's words again. *Don't expect Trentham to marry you.*

She knew there was no chance of that. Instead she would have to be as

120

polite to Mr Burnley as possible. She expected that evening to be the most excruciating torture and could not believe her luck when Trentham happened to sit near her and engaged Mr Burnley in a political discussion.

Mysteriously, Mr Burnley did not appear at dinner the next day. Her father must have asked the question that was tormenting her, because she suddenly heard Mrs Gregory announce, 'Oh, but he received an urgent letter from London and left an hour ago.'

The party had thus diminished and as a result, Trentham found Eleanor Seymour was sitting closer to him than usual. He wondered if she knew that it was whispered by some that Mr Burnley had gone to London to have his marriage settlements drawn up, and by others that he had broken off the connection altogether.

If Trentham had been asked to take sides, he would have chosen the latter. That morning he had forced himself to sit down and write his business letters, but he had not been making much progress. When the door opened, he looked up with a frown. It was Mr Burnley and he strove to clear his face.

'I thought I ought to inform you, sir,' Mr Burnley said. 'Something has come up and I have to return to town directly.'

Trentham expressed polite concern, but his eyes were observant. Mr Burnley was not a happy man. The obvious conclusion was that Miss Seymour had not been able to bring herself to say yes to his proposal. Burnley's next words served to strengthen this suspicion.

'Be careful not to get your fingers burned. I've seen the way you look at a certain young lady. She's not as young and innocent as she pretends to be.'

Trentham thanked him dryly, pretending not to understand what he meant. But it made him question what his intentions were towards Eleanor.

Later, he was glad when he could

leave the dining-room, where a raucous group had gathered, and return to the drawing-room, but even there he felt distracted. His eyes kept drifting towards Eleanor. He wanted to sit with her, talk to her, but it would excite gossip.

He couldn't help remembering the way she smiled as she danced, her red cheeks at the lakeside, her attempts to shield Mary when he caught them on the stairs. The child was fond of her and talked about Miss Seymour whenever she had the opportunity. But Eleanor didn't flirt with him or offer herself as a potential mother to Mary, and that troubled him.

The slam of the door made everyone look up. Harriet Reed stopped in the middle of a song as Louisa Alcock sailed into the centre of the room, her lips twisted into a triumphant smile. A murmur ran round the room, but no-one moved. Trentham was the first to recover.

'Miss Alcock,' he said, slowly and

deliberately, 'this is an unexpected pleasure. I assume you came to see me. Shall we step into the library?'

Louisa turned her head towards him, but her expression did not alter.

'I have nothing to say to you, James Trentham, that cannot be said in front of your friends.'

The poisonous whisper caused a stir among the company. They all felt they ought to go, but fascination kept them captive. Trentham lifted his head and fire sparkled in his eyes, but he made an effort to remain calm.

'For your sake, I think it would be better if we talked privately.'

'So you can deny my existence and then marry some rich girl and pretend you never loved me?'

The blood rushed to his face. He crossed his arms to stop himself from bustling Louisa out of the room. Such behaviour would only serve to confirm her accusations.

'Why don't you sit down, Miss Alcock?'

This invitation seemed to confuse Louisa. She glanced around her for the first time. Mr Seymour, who had been hovering nearby, hastily offered her a chair. She shook her head, obviously feeling it would put her at a disadvantage, but sensing a potential ally, she grabbed him by the sleeve.

'I know you,' she said. 'You'll take my part, won't you? You said you had a daughter.'

'Yes.' Mr Seymour glanced uncertainly at Trentham.

'Do you think it right that a man should inveigle himself into the heart of an innocent girl and then abandon her?'

Mr Seymour's glance again appealed to Trentham for help, but Louisa seemed not to notice his hesitation.

'It isn't right,' she declared. 'You cannot deny it, can you?'

'What precisely do you accuse me of?' Trentham asked.

He could feel prickles of unease. Perhaps by taking this risk, he could reveal to the others how misguided

Louisa was. But it might backfire if they took her part.

'Don't you remember how we met? You wrapped me in your coat and carried me all the way home, whispering the sweetest, kindest words in my ear. I will never, never forget it.'

'Miss Alcock, you had nearly drowned. If I hadn't wrapped you up, you might have caught your death. And as for what I said, I was afraid that if you lost consciousness, you might slip into death.'

Her face blossomed.

'I knew it. I knew you loved me from the moment you first laid eyes on me. You could not bear to see me die.'

She was twisting his words. He finally lost his temper.

'Do you think I would have let you drown if you had been old and ugly? I never felt anything for you but compassion.'

Her lips began to tremble, but she shook her head.

'No, it's not true. Why are you lying?'

Trentham stopped. He didn't want to humiliate her in public. His eye accidentally fell on Eleanor and she hastily averted her head. Could he bring himself to marry Louisa Alcock out of pity?

'Please, come with me into the library. We'll discuss the matter there.'

'Why? I already know what you want to say to me.'

'I don't believe you do,' he said very gently, as he laid his hand on her arm. 'You are not well. Let me ring for the carriage to take you home.'

'Don't patronise me, as if I were a child. Tell them. Tell her you are going to marry me.'

She ripped herself free and pointed an accusing finger at Eleanor.

'You're the one who seduced him away from me. But you won't prevail.'

'I assure you . . . ' Eleanor began, her cheeks scarlet.

A gasp shot across the room. Louisa had pulled a dagger out of the bodice of her gown. Trentham took a step back, his eyes fixed on her. He was the only person in the room, perhaps, who could persuade her to give up her weapon.

'Louisa, this will achieve nothing. Think what this will do to your family.'

'If I can't have you, no-one will.'

Trentham could see her hand tightly clasping the dagger, as if nerving herself to the deed. It was dangerous, but he decided to call her bluff.

'Very well. If you think it will solve anything, there'll be no buttons to hinder you this time.'

He tore open his coat and waistcoat. From a vast distance, he heard a button roll along the floorboards beyond the carpet. His eyes locked on Louisa's. She raised her hand for the blow, but she was trembling violently. There were tears in her eyes, as well as fury and pain. He saw the muscles in her shoulder tense. She was really going to do it. Instinctively, Trentham drew in his breath, waiting.

'Stop, in heaven's name!'

It was Eleanor's voice. Out of the

whole assembly, she was the only one to leap forward and snatch Louisa by the wrist. The tears vanished from Louisa's eyes. Only hatred remained. Eleanor was in far graver peril then he had ever been, Trentham realised with sickening certainty. Love and conscience had withheld Louisa till now, but she had no such feelings towards her rival.

'You are right,' she hissed, 'this is a much better plan.'

Eleanor's fingers tightened on her wrist.

'Listen to me first. I renounce all claim to Mr Trentham's affections. He is yours, if he will have you.'

'Is this some sort of trick?'

'Louisa, please,' Trentham intervened. 'Before all these witnesses, I swear I have no intention of marrying Miss Seymour.'

Louisa's arm sank by her side and slipped out of Eleanor's grip.

'Give me the dagger,' Trentham murmured.

She uttered a little crooning noise

and began to sway.

'Eleanor, child, come away.'

Mr Seymour put his arms round his daughter. Louisa's eyes flashed up at the sound of his voice.

'That is your daughter?' she croaked.

'Yes.'

Her swaying grew more pronounced. Trentham was certain she would fall, but the knife was still in her loosened grip. He had to be wary for Eleanor's sake, if not his own.

'Oh, heavens, what a conspiracy,' Louisa muttered in the rapid undertone that always denoted agitation. 'I thought you were my friend, when all the while you were plotting against me to rob me of the man I love.'

'Eleanor, be careful!' Trentham cried out, seeing the renewed glare in Louisa's eyes.

'So you do love her after all.'

With a howl of anguish, Louisa lunged forward, then backed away as Trentham interposed himself between her and the Seymours. She struck against the wall.

'Cornered like a rat,' she muttered. 'They all plotted against me, all told lies about me and you believed them. But I'll show you how a true woman can die.'

The blade flashed in the candlelight across one wrist, then the other. It happened so suddenly, Trentham was powerless to prevent it. The dagger clattered to the floor as he took her by both hands, her blood seeping through his fingers.

'Louisa, what have you done?'

'She shall never triumph over me,' she whispered as she laid her head upon his breast. 'Now I can die content.'

8

Everything seemed very confused after that. Eleanor was pushed aside as the others called the servants, sent for the doctor and helped Trentham convey Louisa upstairs.

Eleanor's knees buckled and she collapsed into the nearest chair, feeling sick and faint. She had never expected to see such hatred directed towards her as she had seen in Louisa's eyes. She had known that, unless she clung hard enough, she might be staring death in the face. But she couldn't stand by and let Trentham confront the madwoman alone.

But the necessity of renouncing all claims to a man who thought her a presumptuous fortune hunter was humiliating. She knew gossip grew from such simple things. People would overlook the fact that a life had been at risk. They would assume there must have been a secret understanding between her and Trentham to explain Louisa's accusations.

The pungent smell of ammonia made her choke and look up. Harriet was holding a reviving bottle under her nose.

'Are you feeling a little better now? Did she hurt you?'

Eleanor shook her head.

'Only my pride is hurt,' she said with a shaky laugh, and then she had another vision of the knife raised against Trentham.

'Let's go to your room,' Harriet suggested. 'They won't miss us there.'

Eleanor nodded. When they were alone, Harriet encouraged her to talk. She had a good cry once the shock had sunk in, which made her feel better. But she couldn't face the rest of the company again. Harriet made sure she had everything she needed before she went to gather the latest news.

'Miss Alcock isn't badly hurt,' she

reported back. 'The doctor has bandaged her arms and she'll have to stay in bed and rest for a while. I'm not sure I should tell you this but they've decided it would be best not to leave her alone, in case she tries to harm herself or anyone else.'

Eleanor shuddered. She had an image of Louisa Alcock creeping along the corridors after everyone was asleep, trying every door until she found her enemy, but she didn't voice her fear to Harriet.

Later her father came to see how she was.

'Can we leave soon, Papa?' she asked him. 'I don't like being in the same house as her.'

Mr Seymour patted her shoulder.

'You have nothing to worry about, Nell. She can't hurt you. If you saw how pale and exhausted she is. She cried herself sick and Mr Trentham talked to her for a good while until she settled.'

So he was going to marry her after

all. What else could have had such a soothing effect? Somehow that made everything seem worse.

'He asked after you, too.'

'What? Who?'

She raised her head, feeling dazed.

'Mr Trentham, of course. He wanted to be sure you had suffered no ill effects from the incident.'

'No, I'll feel better after a good night's sleep,' Eleanor said heavily, though she didn't add that she might not be able to sleep for weeks.

It was with some trepidation that she left her room the following morning. Louisa's door was near the head of the stairs and she crept past it as quickly and quietly as possible, as if she was afraid Louisa might recognise her footsteps. She knew she was being silly, but she couldn't help herself.

She was surprised by how much concern the other guests showed towards her. Trentham entered the room shortly before breakfast. He had a preoccupied air and his eyes ran swiftly across the room as if he were searching for someone in particular. His face lit up as he caught sight of Eleanor and he began crossing the room towards her, but he was intercepted by someone else wanting to know the latest news.

'I've sent word to Miss Alcock's family,' he said. 'The doctor seems to think she is well enough to travel, though he had to give her laudanum last night to make sure she slept soundly.'

The day passed quietly. The frivolity and carelessness had gone and people spent a good deal of time whispering in corners. Despite reassurances about how subdued Louisa was, Eleanor felt uneasy in the house and in the afternoon she set out for a solitary walk.

Somehow she found herself in the summerhouse by the lake and she sat down to rest. She let her hands slide into her lap and closed her eyes. She was so tired after her poor night, she could almost have fallen asleep.

She had to get away from this place soon. She couldn't stay in the same house as Louisa, not if she was going to marry Trentham.

An unexpected noise startled her out of her reverie.

'I beg your pardon, Miss Seymour, I didn't mean to alarm you.'

James Trentham was hovering on the top step of the summerhouse.

'You have more right to be here than I do,' she replied.

That settled his doubts. He came fully into the summerhouse and sat down next to her, placing his hat on the seat beside him. Eleanor noticed beads of sweat on his forehead, where the brim of his hat had rested, and a light down of dust on his green coat.

'It's rather hot for riding,' he said, confirming her conjecture.

'I can imaginc. Estate business, I suppose?'

'No. I have had a good deal to think about.'

'That's why I came here,' she

137

confessed with a shy smile.

Trentham looked down at his hands.

'I didn't have an opportunity to ask how you were last night after your ordeal,' he said, a little awkwardly.

'I am perfectly well, thank you.'

He scanned her face for signs of fatigue, as if he didn't quite believe her. She blushed, but she couldn't tear her eyes away from his. Tentatively he took her hand.

'That was a very brave and, dare I say it, rash thing to do,' he said.

'I know. But I couldn't bear to see you hurt.'

She blurted out the truth before she could stop herself. There was an awkward silence.

'I suppose you think I ought to marry her and spare her feelings.'

'It's none of my business,' Eleanor replied.

She was surprised how numb her lips felt. She knew some people would think it was the honourable thing to do, but she felt an unspeakable repugnance at the thought of Trentham marrying Louisa Alcock.

'Tell me, if the positions were reversed, if I loved her and she didn't care tuppence for me, would you still advocate marriage? No, I thought not. You would cry out at the cruelty of forcing a young woman into a loveless marriage, especially when . . . '

He broke off suddenly. Eleanor looked up. He was gazing at her intently. His lips seemed very close to hers, and for a moment she thought he would kiss her. An apologetic cough from the doorway made them both jump.

'Mr Alcock has just arrived at the house, sir,' Mr Seymour announced. 'I assumed you would wish to speak to him at the first opportunity.'

Eleanor could see the gleam in his eye as he observed them. She bristled. This time she would nip her father's rumour-mongering in the bud.

Mr Trentham bowed at her and murmured an excuse.

Eleanor saw her father was about to follow and she called out, 'Could I speak with you a moment, Papa?'

'What is it, child?'

'It's a matter of utmost importance.'

Reluctantly, he returned to the summerhouse. His eye fell on Mr Trentham's hat, still lying on the bench where he had left it.

'Well, well, make haste.'

'Papa, I don't want you to misinterpret my being here alone with Mr Trentham. It happened quite by chance.'

'Perhaps that is true on your side, Nell, but can you be sure of his?'

'No, Papa, I am tired of this. I don't want you to add fuel to any rumours about me and Mr Trentham. There is not the slightest hope of marriage.'

'You seem to forget I am your father.'

'I mean it, Papa. I'll ask Mrs Reed to find me a place as a governess, if that is the only way to support myself, but I won't pretend I am engaged to Mr Trentham. Not after all that has happened.'

Eleanor hurtled down the steps and along the path leading away from the house. She was unaware that in the still, summer air, her voice had carried and James Trentham, having returned for his hat, had heard every word of her last speech.

He barely managed to draw into the shadows, but if she had gone in the opposite direction, a meeting would have been inevitable. As it was, he only hesitated for a second before setting off towards the house. He didn't want Seymour to catch him loitering. And he could not keep Mr Alcock waiting any longer.

The house was in turmoil when Eleanor returned. She had walked and walked until she was exhausted. She was surprised to find Trentham's coach on the drive and as she passed the library, a servant came out with the remains of a meal. Through the open door, Eleanor glimpsed Trentham and a stranger sitting opposite each other, frowning.

'Where have you been?' Harriet asked, as soon as she entered the drawing-room. 'We were just about to send out a search party.'

'Has anything happened while I have been out?'

'Nobody seems to know,' Harriet replied and drew her into a quiet corner and dropped her voice. 'There's some sort of delay. I'm pretty sure Mr Trentham went upstairs to see Miss Alcock, after the doctor asked to speak to him, and now he has been in the library with her father for heaven knows how long. There have been raised voices, too.'

She stopped abruptly when the door opened and Trentham strode in. He was still dressed in his riding coat, his hat under his arm. Eleanor could see it was not just anxiety that made him so pale. He was angry, too. His eyes swept the room, but Eleanor got the impression he saw nothing.

'It seems,' he began, 'Miss Alcock refuses to leave unless I go, too, so I shall be forced to leave you to entertain yourselves in my absence. I trust I will only be gone for twenty-four hours at the most.'

A murmur of sympathy went around the room. He shook hands with those nearest to him, but he seemed anxious to be gone. Eleanor remained in the shadows. Through the open door, she could see a huddled figure being led down the stairs, half-hidden behind the stranger who had been in the library. Mr Trentham bowed and withdrew, and a moment later she heard the carriage pull away from the front of the house.

Outwardly the house did not change on that first day. Like a well-oiled, well-wound clock, everything proceeded just as it had the previous day. The company dressed for dinner, spent the evening together, retired for the night. The next day, meals were eaten at regular intervals, walks were taken, conversations initiated, music practised. But towards evening, the sense of anticipation grew. Mr Trentham neither returned, nor sent word.

The evening's entertainment fell flat. Some sat up late, speculating on what might have happened. Others went to their rooms early but did not sleep. Unease was gradually descending on the house.

The next morning brought a letter from Trentham, which one of the guests read out over breakfast. The situation had turned out to be more complicated than Trentham had anticipated and as a result he would have to extend his absence for an indefinite period.

He reiterated that they were welcome to stay at Deepwater as long as they chose, but after breakfast, preparations began for the exodus. A much smaller party assembled at dinner than had gathered at breakfast. Those still there had not been able to obtain horses or they knew the right coach would not pass through Nottingham for a day or two.

Eleanor and her father were among those. As soon as Trentham's letter arrived, she had tried to talk to her father but she was unable to get near him. He was much too busy, making inquiries about horses, coaches and all manner of other matters on behalf of other guests. Instead she contented herself with gathering together her possessions, packing.

Harriet was among the first to leave and Mrs Gregory followed soon afterwards. The empty seats in her carriage, however, were given to another family travelling in the same direction. Eleanor could not help feeling alarmed. Evidently they would not be able to leave the same way they had come. Even Mary had gone, as Mr Trentham had asked a female friend to deliver her to her new school.

By the second evening, Eleanor's suspicions were growing that her father was avoiding her. Only once she overheard someone ask her father about his plans.

'Oh, we shall do capitally. I've written to a friend to make some arrangements and we'll be gone as soon as I receive a reply.'

Eleanor got no explanation when she did catch him alone.

'Trust me, Nell. I have everything in hand.'

'Where are we going? When are we leaving?'

'Leaving?' he murmured, looking vague. 'Oh, tomorrow, I daresay.'

'In the morning, the afternoon?'

'Hm? Oh, yes, yes, most likely. Excuse me, I've just remembered something.'

He disappeared before she could stop him.

Their numbers were reduced still further at breakfast the next morning. Eleanor gathered some people had risen at dawn and left then. Those still there were mostly close friends or relatives of the absent host, save for the Seymours. Eleanor didn't like feeling like an intruder. As the lowliest guests there, they should have been the first to go.

After breakfast she packed the

remainder of her possessions. She would give her father no excuse to delay their departure. When there was nothing left to do, she wandered downstairs. The house seemed to echo with the sound of trunk lids banging, keys turning, boxes thumping down the stairs, horses pawing the ground and the clatter of wheels. Eleanor did not see her father all morning. She tried reading, but the atmosphere was too unsettled. She loitered on the steps, waving goodbye to people she knew only slightly and took herself for a lonely walk along the drive to the gatehouse. She almost ran back, afraid she had been away too long.

There was no carriage on the wide expanse of the drive, nor any sign of her father or anyone else in the house. For an uncanny moment, she felt as if she had been forgotten, left behind like a broken toy when the children had departed. Wandering into the garden, she came across an elderly couple, the last guests left at

Deepwater Hall.

'Are you still here then, my dear?' the old lady asked politely.

'I'm afraid so. My father was waiting for an important letter.'

'I daresay the servants will send it on if you leave the address.'

'Yes, of course,' Eleanor replied as brightly as she could.

She left them soon afterwards, feeling she was in their way. They were to leave just after the early dinner that had been ordered for the remnants of the party. Mr Seymour only appeared as they were sitting down to eat and conducted a boisterous conversation, which seemed too loud for the rather empty dining-room.

Eleanor watched the departure of the elderly couple as if they were the last friends she had left on earth. If she had asked them, would they have taken them to the nearest coaching-inn? It was too late to wonder now. The long-awaited letter had arrived at dinner and her father disappeared with it as soon as the meal was over.

She had no way of guessing how long Trentham might be away. Suppose he was on his way back already? Suppose he had given way to their persuasions and married Louisa and he would bring her back as his bride. She would die of mortification if he caught her here, taking advantage of his hospitality so shamelessly.

Even if they managed to leave before he returned, she didn't know how she would face Mr Trentham again. The servants would tell him they were the last to go. Suddenly determined, she searched all the reception rooms and discovered her father in the library, at Mr Trentham's desk, using his host's pen and ink as naturally as if they were his own.

'What is it, child?' he asked, irritably. 'Close the door. It's causing a draught.'

Eleanor reluctantly shut the door, but stayed standing next to it. A feeling of complicity in something she objected to overwhelmed her.

'Papa, I need to know when we are leaving. I have a right to know.'

Mr Seymour frowned. 'It's not good news, Eleanor. Something I hoped for has not turned out the way I wished.'

'But there must be something we can do, somewhere we can go.'

'Without money?'

'None?'

He smiled wryly, but said nothing.

'But we cannot stay here,' she wailed, suddenly feeling trapped.

'No, no, of course not. We'll go back to London. There's a coach in two days' time. But you'd better make up your mind to marry Mr Burnley. There is no other choice left.'

And with that he turned back to his letter.

Hours crept by. Unable to settle, Eleanor wandered about the garden until it became too dark. Her appetite dwindled. She had no right to be there, but suddenly she was afraid of what would happen when she left.

The place felt so desolate, she could

have cried. She spent a lot of time in the summerhouse, brooding until she was sick of her own thoughts. She cried herself asleep at night, making wild plans about running away and forcing her father to follow. She had been compelled to unpack the bare minimum of her possessions. At all sorts of odd hours, she thought she heard hooves pounding or carriage wheels crunching, only to discover it was a trick of her imagination.

She paid little heed, therefore, when she heard them again as she was getting ready for yet another walk the following afternoon. She had just reached the foot of the stairs when the front door sprang open. She started and glanced up for an instant, but a glance was all she needed to realise the master of the house had returned.

9

Eleanor saw the surprise in his eyes, but not the gleam of pleasure that succeeded it. His first instinct was to start forward, as she shrank into the shadows. Her face grew scarlet and she felt certain she would never be able to look him in the eye again.

'Miss Seymour,' he said, his voice low and uncharacteristically gentle, 'I did not expect to find you still here.'

'No, I — my father — ' she stammered herself to a halt as she curtsied.

Too late she noticed his hand outstretched in friendship. She would have tried to rectify her mistake, but he withdrew his hand and bowed instead.

Afraid he might be offended, she attempted to look up at him, but her eyes would go no higher than his mouth. Its corners were twitching, as if he was choosing his next words carefully.

'Of course you are welcome to stay as long as you choose,' he said, still in that softened tone. 'You were about to take a walk, I perceive?'

'Yes, sir.'

'I shall not detain you then.'

He opened the door for her and she muttered her thanks in barely audible tones. It was all she could do not to burst into a run until she was out of sight. Before she turned the corner, she glanced back and found he was watching her from the half-open door.

That glance brought James Trentham to his senses. Without a word to the servants, he went into the library and leaned against the door. For a moment, he shut his eyes, trying to breathe deeply, and when he opened them, he was rewarded by the sight of Eleanor flying across the lawn towards the shelter of the summerhouse.

He knew it was just visible from his dressing-room window. Careless of appearances, he leaped up the stairs, two at a time, crashing through the door, pressing himself against the window frame. The slender figure ran up the steps of the summerhouse and, just before she vanished from his sight, he saw her cover her heated face with both hands. He could imagine the low moan she must have uttered, because something similar escaped from his own lips.

What he would not have given to be in the summerhouse with her, to peel her hands gently away from her face and kiss her, before drawing her into his arms and tucking her head under his chin so she could hide her hot cheeks against the lapels of his coat.

The days and hours away from her had revealed to him how much he was in love with her. The slightest movement would make him catch his breath, convinced she was nearby. He realised now how much time he had spent over the past weeks, hoping to see her, to sit near her, to hear her voice, even if he was too far away to catch her words.

At night, he lay awake, bitterly regretting every harsh word he had uttered in her hearing. By day the very nature of his arguments with the Alcocks had fixed Eleanor more indelibly in his mind. How could he be expected to sacrifice himself to one woman's obsession, when he could not stop thinking about another? And, worst of all, he had no reason to believe Eleanor returned his feelings.

It was only as he was travelling home that he allowed his imagination to run riot. He imagined what it would be like to step into the hall and see her flying down the staircase to meet him, face glowing with pleasure, her arms outstretched, whereas he knew in stark reality, he would find the house abandoned and echoing with memories of her.

So vividly had he imagined the scene, that he had instinctively sprung forward to kiss her when her face was, indeed, the first sight he saw on returning home. Her air of embarrassment quickly brought him to his senses and he could have bitten out his tongue when he saw his thoughtless words made her feel her humiliating position more keenly.

He forced himself downstairs again. He could not stand there, watching, waiting, longing for her to come back. He rang the bell for the butler and managed to ask in casual tones if there had been any trouble while he was away.

'No, sir, none that I can think of. There are only two guests remaining, Mr Seymour and his daughter.'

'I hope you have made them comfortable,' Trentham ventured.

The butler allowed his eye to flicker momentarily.

'Mr Seymour has availed himself of every comfort in the house,' he said, disapproval palpable in his voice. 'Miss Seymour is no trouble whatsoever. Her maid says her trunk has been packed since the day after you left, sir, and she spends much of her time wandering about the grounds.'

Involuntarily, Trentham's eyes moved to the window. As far as he knew, she was still in the summerhouse, fighting with her shame, nerving herself for the moment when she would have to return to the house.

If it would spare her feelings, he almost wished he could find some excuse to leave the house. Since that was impossible without causing raised eyebrows, he must do the next best thing — grit his teeth and treat her father with a respect he did not deserve, simply because he was her father.

He dismissed the butler and sought out his half-welcome guest. If this was the price for having Eleanor in his house, he was willing to pay it. For her sake, Trentham bore with Mr Seymour's servility as he congratulated him on the swift completion of his task with the Alcocks. From the hints he dropped, Trentham could tell Seymour was dying to know what had happened, but he refused to gratify him.

Seymour had, it seemed, a vague consciousness that he had no right to be there, since he made some excuse about the London coach being full, thus preventing them from departing any sooner.

'We will leave tomorrow after breakfast,' he promised.

Trentham felt his heart grow numb. So soon? Through an effort of will, he managed not to say the words out loud. Eleanor would not thank him for it, and her feelings were paramount at present.

A cold sweat ran over him at the thought she might find some excuse not to join them at dinner. But he had reckoned without Eleanor's dislike of causing unnecessary trouble and therefore she did not ask for a tray to be brought up to her room.

He was horrified by the way she picked at her food, silent, her eyes downcast, trying in every way to disappear from the face of the earth.

'Do have a little more chicken,' he

urged her. 'Look how tender it is.'

'You are very kind, sir, but . . . '

'I shall be mortally offended if you don't try a little. And it will all go to waste if you don't.'

That was not true. She knew perfectly well the servants would eat anything that was left over. But she managed a pale smile and he took it as encouragement to lay the white sliver of meat on her plate. She felt his eyes watching her anxiously, tenderly, so she ate, though everything tasted like sawdust.

'I forgot to mention, I went to see Mary on my way back,' he said.

'How is she?'

'She was a little tearful at parting, but she has made a few friends already. She sent you her love.'

'Be sure to send her mine when you write.'

As the meal drew to a close, Trentham pushed back his chair.

'I think we will forgo our port tonight if you have no objection, sir,' he said. 'I should not like to think of Miss Seymour sitting in the drawing-room alone.'

Eleanor could see her father was not entirely pleased with this arrangement, but he agreed without a murmur. She was afraid Mr Trentham might ask her to play the harpsichord. Her nerves could not have stood it. Instead, he engaged her father in a game of chess and allowed her to sit sewing quietly. She felt humbled by Trentham's kindness. She had expected him to show his disapproval in no uncertain terms and she didn't quite trust this transformation.

When at last it was late enough to go to bed, he rose and opened the door for her.

'I wanted to apologise for all the unjust things I have said to you in the past,' he said in low tones. 'I hope you will forgive me.'

'Of course,' she replied and, to her surprise, she discovered it was true.

Her heart suddenly felt lighter and

then she remembered she was leaving in the morning and her father was threatening her with marriage to Mr Burnley. And something even heavier oppressed her spirits, something she did not want to put into words.

She woke early and lay for a good while in bed, wondering if Trentham had gone for a swim in the icy waters of the lake. She knew it was foolish, thinking of him in that way, but she couldn't help herself. The whole house seemed different now he was back. She dreaded, yet longed to see him again. She found him in the drawing-room. A newspaper was spread out on the table before him, but his head was turned so he could gaze out of the window. He started as she took a step forward.

'I hope I am not intruding,' she ventured.

'Not at all.'

She forced herself to say the next words.

'I trust Miss Alcock has recovered fully.'

He wouldn't meet her eyes.

'Her health has been restored,' he said. 'I cannot say the same for her peace of mind.'

'Cannot you bring yourself to return her affection?'

'I pity her. But I am frightened I may grow to resent her in time.'

Eleanor knew she had no right to question him further. To her surprise, he went on.

'Her parents are offering me an obscene amount of money if I will marry her, though, God knows, I am rich enough already.'

'What will you do?' she asked shyly, afraid he would think she was prying.

'I have no idea.'

They didn't seem to have anything more to say to one another, judging from the silence that followed. Eleanor stole a glance at Trentham, only to find his eyes resting on her meditatively. He gave her a wry smile.

'So you see, I can now sympathise better with your dilemma concerning

Mr Burnley. Is it true your father owes him a considerable sum of money?'

Eleanor's fingers clenched tightly. She could barely sit still. The truth, then, had come out, for all her father's pretences. She knew he would have told her to deny everything, but she could not bring herself to do it.

'I am not in my father's confidence,' she said.

'I know I have no right to interfere, but if I can be of any assistance . . . '

'Thank you. I don't suppose you know anyone in need of a governess?'

He smiled ruefully. 'If I had known sooner that you were looking for a position, I would not have sent Mary to school.'

Somehow this was unbearable. She began to pace the room. To be relegated from the least important guest to what was in effect an upper servant made her writhe.

'Of course there is one other solution,' Trentham began cautiously.

'Indeed? I wish you would tell me.'

The smile on his lips looked forced.

'You could marry me,' he said.

Her heart thudded in the silent room. Why had she never realised before that she was in love with him? At lightning speed a thousand images darted through her head. She had only to say yes and she would be cradled safely in his arms. Except . . .

He looked grave enough, but it couldn't be true. He had made no mention of love. Perhaps he thought she was the solution to his problem with the Alcocks. Or was he simply making fun of her or testing her? She tightened her lips, fighting the sudden urge to cry.

'I'm afraid I don't find your little jest amusing,' Eleanor said, drawing herself up to her full height.

She could see conflicting emotions cross his face, as if he could not decide whether to persist or not.

'I apologise,' he said quietly. 'You are quite right. It was in poor taste.'

Eleanor swallowed, but mercifully she

was spared the need to reply by the entrance of her father.

★   ★   ★

It was late the following evening when they arrived in London. Numbed by the shaking of the stagecoach and long hours spent brooding over her last interview with Trentham, Eleanor did not question what they were going to do there.

Trentham's carriage had taken them as far as Nottingham and she wondered how a man could simultaneously show so much and so little consideration. He had seemed so kind since his return. Why had he spoiled it all by that mock-proposal?

Of course she need not have taken it so much to heart. She could see now that she ought to have laughed it off. He probably thought her gawky and unsophisticated, and telling herself his opinion was of no importance didn't help.

Eleanor was jolted out of her absorption when the hack stopped outside their town house. It seemed larger than ever and smelled as musty as if it had been abandoned for years. Most of the furniture was swathed up and Eleanor gathered her father only intended to stay there until he could coax an invitation out of one of his patrons.

While they were picking over a meagre breakfast the following morning, there was a knock at the front door and Mr Burnley was shown into the dining-room.

'My dear fellow, so good of you to come,' Mr Seymour exclaimed, shaking hands with the older man heartily.

'You made it sound like a matter of urgency, and I am always willing to oblige a friend.'

Although his words were pleasant, his tone was stiff. There was less infatuation and more determination in his face than previously. Eleanor excused herself as soon as she could. The fact that they let her go suggested they were eager to get to business.

Sure enough some thirty minutes later, the message came that her father wished to speak to her in the library. Mr Burnley was examining the pictures with a proprietorial air. Seymour, on the other hand, looked ill at ease. He rose, but Eleanor barred his exit.

'I would rather you stayed, Papa.'

'What is this nonsense, Eleanor?'

Guilt made him irritable. He turned to his guest.

'I must apologise, sir, for my daughter's strange behaviour.'

Mr Burnley laughed unconvincingly.

'Oh, think nothing of it. Young ladies must have their whims, mustn't they?' But as an afterthought, he added, 'Perhaps you should stay. Miss Seymour may be more amenable to you than she is to me.'

Mr Seymour bowed and took the initiative.

'You are a very fortunate girl, Eleanor. There are not many men as generous as Mr Burnley.'

The guest visibly expanded at this praise. Eleanor bit her tongue. If she spoke too soon she would be scolded for being forward.

'In short, he has asked for your hand in marriage.'

'In exchange for discharging your debts? I'm sorry, Papa, but I cannot consent to being sold to the highest bidder as if I were the second-best china.'

Her father glanced nervously at Mr Burnley, afraid he might take offence.

'You must learn to curb your tongue, child,' he began, but Eleanor interrupted.

'I am not a child. You cannot bully me. I would willingly go out and teach, or scrub floors, or sell flowers in the streets, but I will not marry for money.'

'Think carefully, before you reject my offer, Miss Seymour,' Mr Burnley intervened. 'I have more power over your family than you think.'

'How very noble of you to use it against us.'

'Do you want your father to go to gaol?'

She willed herself not to cry. The memory of James Trentham haunted her. If his proposal had been genuine, she could have defied Mr Burnley and saved her father at the same time.

'You really have no choice in the matter,' Mr Burnley persisted.

'Papa?'

She gazed at him, her eyes begging him to save her. He turned aside. She couldn't bear to stay in the library a moment longer. She pushed past her father and stumbled up the stairs to her bedroom. She hid there, waiting for the sound of the front door. Her heart sank when she heard her father's steps approach her room.

'May I come in, Eleanor?'

She rose and opened the door in silence. She had expected her father to be in a towering rage, but instead he looked tired and defeated.

'Please, Papa, I would do a great deal for you, but please, don't make me marry him. I could never be happy with him.'

'I know, Eleanor. I've sent him away. Heaven alone knows what will become of us now. I had such hopes Trentham would propose before we left Notting-hamshire.'

Her heart throbbed. Suppose, suppose . . .

'You realise we must leave London immediately?'

'Do you mean . . . '

He nodded.

'I have unpacked nothing since last night,' she said. 'If we sent for a hack, we could be gone in a matter of minutes.'

But they were already too late. When the footman opened the door to fetch a cab, two burly men burst in. Eleanor did not need anyone to tell her who they were.

10

The house seemed far too empty to Trentham. Rather than fill it with people he didn't wish to see, he accepted the first invitation he received, hoping to meet Eleanor or at least hear news of her.

He had been a fool to let her go like that. He should have fought harder to persuade her he was in earnest. Uncertainty gnawed at him. Did she feel anything for him? She had risked her life to save him, but had it been out of compassion?

It was not till his second evening at Bath that he overheard someone ask, 'What on earth has become of that cat's-paw, Seymour? I laid a wager he'd be here with his pretty, little daughter.'

'Haven't you heard? He got himself arrested for debt in London. A bad business. Burnley bought up all his debts and this is his revenge because the little filly wouldn't marry him.'

Trentham felt as if he had been run through with a sword. He missed the next sentence and by the time he forced himself to concentrate, the two young sparks had drifted on to a different subject.

If Eleanor was in trouble, he could not stay here, living in luxury. He had to make sure she had some means of support, somewhere to live, someone to help her.

He made up an excuse and left the next morning. He found bailiffs in possession of Mr Seymour's house and he did not care to ask them for details. Instead he did what he ought to have done in the first place and went to consult his lawyer.

Preliminary inquiries established that Mr Seymour's debts were substantial for someone with almost no income, though Trentham could have discharged them without much trouble. He began negotiations to have the matter settled anonymously, though he knew Mr Burnley would resist being deprived of his power over the Seymours. He couldn't let Eleanor's father rot in prison.

Approaching Eleanor herself was a much more delicate matter. He didn't want her to feel grateful or think that he had cynically exploited her predicament. It took time and patience to discover her humble lodgings above a grocer's shop. She had written to Mrs Gregory, giving an address where a reply might reach her, and he traced her from that.

It was not with the intention of seeing her that he wandered into the obscure part of town where she lived. It was purely to make sure she was staying in a decent house that he drifted into the correct street. And when he thought he glimpsed a pale face at a window, he had to go into the shop, in case she had seen him.

He decided against sending up his name, but the grocer's wife took one look at his well-cut coat and showed him into what was evidently the best room in the house.

He had gone into Eleanor's room at Deepwater, after she left, and thought it was humble enough, but this was far, far worse. She was a proud woman. How would she bear his intrusion? But he had come too far to go back.

He seemed to wait for hours in the cramped parlour, listening to the neighbours quarrelling. His agitation grew as he recognised Eleanor's step on the uncarpeted stairs, slower and heavier than before. He turned his back to the door, to conceal his emotion. In a sudden panic, he realised he had thought of nothing to say to her.

'You wished to see me, sir?' she asked, stopping just inside the door.

She started visibly as he turned towards her. If he had not been watching so intently, he might have missed the incredulous smile that flitted across her face.

'Forgive me, Miss Seymour. I didn't

mean to take you by surprise. How are you?'

He could see for himself that she was pale and listless, but she insisted that she was well. Her fingers grasped the knot of the shawl that covered her shoulders. She looked at him uncertainly as if afraid he might crush her at any moment.

'How much does my father owe you?' she croaked, barely audibly.

'Nothing. And I would not take a penny from you, Eleanor, if he did.'

Unexpectedly, he found he was standing beside her, pressing her hands to try to reassure her. It was almost the first time he had allowed himself to utter her name, but he was not sure if she noticed. Her head drooped to avoid his gaze, but she did not pull her hands free. They lay passively in his grasp, as if she was undecided what to do next.

'That is very generous, but despite what people say, my father is a man of honour.'

She raised her head with a sudden

resurgence of pride.

'You need not be afraid to tell me. I'll see to it that you are paid, if you are willing to wait.'

'It's an attitude that does you credit. But if anyone is in debt it is I. You saved my life. I came because I was afraid I would never see you again.'

'It's better this way,' she began, but her voice wavered.

He could see tears in her eyes and for the first time he felt hope.

'Have you any plans for the future?'

'I've placed an advertisement offering my services as a governess.'

She bit her lip to stop it from trembling. The advertisement had cost her more than she could easily spare at present, and if there were no replies, she could not afford to repeat the experiment. She slid her fingers out of his cool grasp. Her hands seemed unaccountably hot. He was too close to her. No wonder she could not think clearly.

'I see,' Trentham said. 'I don't

suppose there is anything I could do to change your mind.'

'About what, sir?'

'Oh, do stop calling me 'sir'. It makes me feel old.'

His voice became softer and more earnest.

'Can't you see I really want to marry you? I am in love with you, Eleanor.'

Her heart suddenly throbbed so painfully, she thought she would faint. She had scarcely eaten or slept since her father's arrest. No wonder she felt ill. Did he really mean it? She glanced up at his face and found her eyes locked in his.

Before Eleanor could protest or resist, Trentham had taken her into his arms, cupping her face between his hands. His lips pressed against hers.

A shiver ran down her spine. She raised her hands to push him away, but instead she found herself clutching his sleeves, feeling the smooth contours of the muscles beneath, wanting the kiss to go on and on.

'No, I can't. Let go of me,' she gasped, barely coherently.

'Don't you love me the least little bit, Eleanor?' he pleaded.

His thumb brushed lightly across her cheek.

'Or is my wealth the only barrier between us?'

She was frightened by the strength of her reaction and she lashed out because of it.

'Are you sure you would not rather have me as your mistress? I am cheap enough at present and you would not have to apologise for your choice in public.'

'What on earth put such an idea into your head?'

She laughed bitterly.

'It's what Mr Burnley wants.'

'He dared make such a proposition to you? I'll kill him.'

He made a sudden rush at the door. Instinctively she cried out and snatched his arm.

'No, don't go.'

'I'll never leave you if you want me to stay.'

He gathered her into his arms and she let him do it. After the weeks of struggling since her father's arrest, it was wonderful to be held like that, knowing she was protected by someone stronger than herself.

'Call me James and I'll stay with you for ever.'

It was too sudden. Eleanor wanted to believe him so much. His name was on her lips when a dreadful thought crossed her mind.

'What about Louisa Alcock? We swore there was nothing between us.'

'It was the truth at the time. An oath extracted by violence is not legally binding.'

'What about moral obligations?'

'Should I allow that poor, deluded girl to blight my life? I won't lie to you. Her father has threatened to sue me for breach of contract if I marry, but I doubt it will come to anything. And even if it did, it's only money.'

Eleanor's head snapped up. He had no idea what it was to need money so badly you dreamed about it at night.

'Tell me, am I just another of the waifs and strays you collect? I don't want your money, Mr Trentham, nor your pity.'

Trentham finally lost his temper. He let go of her and suddenly she felt very small and alone.

'Well, that's as well, since you're not going to get either. I don't pity you, I admire you, all except that stubborn pride that won't accept help when you need it.'

And with that he stormed out of the room.

'James.'

The word was little more than a gasp. He didn't seem to hear. Stricken, Eleanor stood still, battling the urge to run into the street and call him over and over again.

Instead, she dashed to the window to take one last look at him. To her surprise, he had neither his own carriage nor a hack with him. He strode off at a rapid pace and then, without warning, halfway down the street, his steps wavered and he glanced back over his shoulder.

Eleanor drew away from the window, afraid he had seen her. Would he turn back or go on? She didn't dare look, but seconds ticked past and nobody came.

That's it, then, she thought. He has given up. I have driven away a man who feels an obligation to his illegitimate niece and a poor, distracted creature like Louisa Alcock.

She forced herself to trudge upstairs to her garret. She felt very tired all of a sudden. It would be a long, long time before she would be able to rest. Every day now must be spent trying to find work. She had already written to Mrs Gregory and Mrs Reed, in the hopes they might know somebody. Contrary to what Trentham had said, she was prepared to swallow some of her pride.

She had two sheets of paper and a

thimbleful of ink left. Perhaps she should try another letter, but how would she pay the postage when the replies came? If they came at all.

She slumped across the packing-case that served as her table, her cheek against the hard, rough surface.

There were footsteps on the stairs. The occupant of the next room, a pale-faced seamstress, must be coming home. The walls of the house were so thin, Eleanor had got used to being able to hear every sound her neighbour made. For the first few days, she had jumped every time she heard an unexpected noise, convinced someone had entered her room.

Perhaps it was because she was so still that the noises seemed louder today. She smiled sadly to herself. She could almost have sworn those cautious steps were in her own room.

As lightly as a dove's wing, a hand settled on her shoulder.

'Eleanor,' his voice was barely above a breath. 'Let me take care of you. Or if you must earn your own way, promise you will marry me when you are out of debt. I'll give away all my money. What good is my wealth when it can't buy me the one thing I want?'

There were tears in her eyes as she turned her head upwards. She reached out towards James Trentham and a moment later she was cradled in his arms.

'I'm so sorry,' she croaked. 'I didn't think you were coming back.'

'I'll always come when you call me.'

'James,' she whispered, closing her eyes, 'James.'

THE END

We do hope that you have enjoyed reading this large print book.

Did you know that all of our titles are available for purchase?

We publish a wide range of high quality large print books including:
Romances, Mysteries, Classics
General Fiction
Non Fiction and Westerns

Special interest titles available in large print are:
The Little Oxford Dictionary
Music Book, Song Book
Hymn Book, Service Book

Also available from us courtesy of Oxford University Press:
Young Readers' Dictionary
(large print edition)
Young Readers' Thesaurus
(large print edition)

For further information or a free brochure, please contact us at:
Ulverscroft Large Print Books Ltd.,
The Green, Bradgate Road, Anstey,
Leicester, LE7 7FU, England.
Tel: (00 44) **0116 236 4325**
Fax: (00 44) **0116 234 0205**

VISIONS OF THE HEART

Christine Briscomb

When property developer Connor Grant contracted Natalie Jensen to landscape the grounds of his large country house near Ashley in South Australia, she was ecstatic. But then she discovered he was acquiring — and ripping apart — great swathes of the town. Her own mother's house and the hall where the drama group met were two of his targets. Natalie was desperate to stop Connor's plans — but she also had to fight the powerful attraction flowing between them.

YESTERDAY'S LOVE

Stella Ross

Jessica's return from Africa to claim her inheritance of 'Simon's Cottage', and take up medicine in her home town, is the signal for her past to catch up with her. She had thought the short affair she'd had with her cousin Kirk twelve years ago a long-forgotten incident. But Kirk's unexpected return to England, on a last-hope mission to save his dying son, sparks off nostalgia. It leads Jessica to rethink her life and where it is leading.